LETTER TO LORD LISZT

OTHER NOVELS BY
MARTIN WALSER
PUBLISHED BY
HOLT, RINEHART AND WINSTON
TRANSLATED BY
LEILA VENNEWITZ

Runaway Horse
The Swan Villa
The Inner Man

LETTER TO
LORD LISZT

A NOVEL BY

MARTIN WALSER

TRANSLATED FROM

THE GERMAN BY

LEILA VENNEWITZ

Holt, Rinehart and Winston NEW YORK

First published in the United States in 1985 by
Holt, Rinehart and Winston, 383 Madison Avenue,
New York, New York 10017.
Published simultaneously in Canada by
Holt, Rinehart and Winston of Canada, Limited.
Originally published in the Federal Republic of
Germany under the title *Brief an Lord Liszt*.

Library of Congress Cataloging in Publication Data
Walser, Martin, 1927–
Letter to Lord Liszt.
Translation of: Brief an Lord Liszt.
I. Title.
PT2685.A48B7513 1985   833'.914   85-844
ISBN: 0-03-071027-8

First American Edition
Designer: Margaret M. Wagner
Printed in the United States of America
1 3 5 7 9 10 8 6 4 2

ISBN 0-03-071027-8

TRANSLATOR'S ACKNOWLEDGMENT

I am deeply grateful to my husband,
William, for his continuing assistance
and advice throughout the work of
this translation.
—*Leila Vennewitz*

LETTER TO LORD LISZT

THE Friday before the Whitsun weekend holiday, at three in the afternoon, Rosi Mutter summoned the department heads for a late meeting. That had never happened before. But the occasion was reason enough. Thiele proclaimed it in a voice meant to sound portentous.

At first he had trouble finding the right words, and he made no effort to disguise the fact that he was having trouble finding the right words. Something had happened that shook Thiele to the core.

. Benedikt Stierle has given up. But the way he did it! Last night he set fire to his plant. And to himself. Beside Stierle's charred body the remains of a rifle had been found. Had Stierle been shot? Investigations were still under way. But Mr. Thiele, to whom everything

was perfectly clear, said: "A typical Stierle solution."
A Benedikt Stierle cannot admit defeat, so he arranges
everything to make it look as if he were the victim of a
crime. Stierle defeated? By Thiele? Never! Stierle, an
ingenious inventor but a hopeless businessman, finds a
solution! He sets fire to his plant in a number of places,
stations himself at the midway point as the fire races
toward the center, and, at the very instant when he
knows for sure that the flames are approaching from all
sides and that the plant is about to collapse over him in
a red-hot mass, he shoots himself.

While Thiele was thus holding forth, Franz Horn
recalled that every summer Thiele spent a week at
Bayreuth. He also recalled that three weeks previously
he had himself written a letter to Benedikt Stierle offering him his services. So his letter had burned up
with Stierle. So he had to go on working here, for
Thiele. Finally Franz Horn also recalled, during this
depiction of the Stierle disaster, what he had attempted
to do four years earlier with some pills—unsuc-
cessfully, as it were. "That nonsense with the pills"
was how he mentally phrased it.

As soon as Franz Horn realized the nature of Thiele's
announcement, he lowered his eyes. Although Thiele
probably wasn't looking at him, Franz Horn looked
away, just in case. He was convinced that Thiele,
while describing Stierle's carefully arranged suicide,
was also thinking of Franz Horn's unsuccessful attempt with the pills. The fact that it had been Thiele
himself who had thwarted the attempt certainly
wouldn't prevent him from including Horn's unsuc-

cessful attempt in the list of Horn's failures. Using the tone of their earliest man-to-man talks, he had once described the sequence of events to Horn. Horn, so Thiele had told him, owed his life to a girl. Nineteen years old. Working in a drugstore. From Tettnang. Shortly before midnight, at the Ravensburg railway station, she had got out of Thiele's car and into her own which, for reasons of discretion, she had parked there. At that moment Thiele catches sight of Horn's car. Very carelessly parked, too, at an angle, taking up almost two parking spaces. He knows it's Horn's car because it used to be his own. Before Thiele started driving those big luxury models, he had often passed on his cars to Horn. To park like that: that's not like Horn! He must have been drunk or something. Anyway, wasn't he supposed to be still in England, negotiating the new license arrangements with Keith Heath in Coventry? What was going on? Surely he can't have left his car parked all askew like that for a whole week! A car parked across the lines like that would be towed away from here the very first day. Something was wrong. If Horn had returned he would have phoned. A man like Horn is always quick to report everything. So Thiele drives out to where Horn lived in those days, on Galgenhalde, notices that the lights are on, is seized by a sharp suspicion, and thus saves his employee's life.

Horn didn't look up until Thiele requested the department heads to rise in honor of their deceased competitor. Thiele said: "I note that you, the department heads of the firms of Chemnitz Dentures and Fin Star, have risen in honor of Benedikt Stierle. I thank you. I wish you a pleasant Whitsuntide."

Never before had Thiele spoken so highly of Benedikt Stierle. Horn could see why. An adversary whom one has finally defeated cannot be sufficiently aggrandized.

Franz Horn was the first to reach the door. Realizing this, he slowed down. But then he wanted to be the first out of the room. Yet he didn't want to admit this. The days when, after such an event, Arthur Thiele would have insisted on exchanging a few words with Franz Horn were over. Franz Horn must not, by leaving slowly, create an impression of wanting to be called back and drawn into conversation. Nor must Dr. Liszt think that Franz Horn was anxious to exchange views on this terrible occurrence. Dr. Liszt— Horn could see this as he hurried out—was evidently even less interested in a conversation with Horn than Horn was in a conversation with Liszt. As soon as Thiele had finished, Dr. Liszt walked toward him. As did Rudolf Ryynänen. As did Dr. Preissker. Obviously Liszt, Ryynänen, and Preissker wanted a chance to discuss Stierle's sensational end with the deeply moved Thiele.

Just as Horn reached the door, he heard Rosi Mutter's cry. Horn looked back and saw Rosi Mutter going down on one knee in front of Thiele and removing a white thread from his dark blue trouser leg. "Mr. Thiele, Mr. Thiele!" she cried. "You're in for a pleasant surprise today—at the very least a kiss!" With that, Horn was outside. Rather than use the elevator he ran down the stairs to his office. He placed some fresh sheets of paper on his desk, which had already been cleared. He kept his secretary mercilessly in the dark as to why Thiele had so unexpectedly summoned the department heads to his office. When Mrs. Brass said good-bye, he pretended to be engrossed in his work, was not to be disturbed, might have to spend the whole of Friday evening here at his desk. He behaved as if, from sheer concentration on his work, he wasn't even properly aware of Mrs. Brass. She mustn't be given the slightest chance of saying she would be glad to stay on if he needed her. Today he felt unable to cope with her Friday afternoon lamentations.

In the years during which Franz Horn had been living apart from his family, Mrs. Brass had developed a solicitude that he now sometimes found irritating. On Fridays she suffered from the fact that they wouldn't be seeing each other again until Monday. And today, because of the long Whitsun weekend, they would be separated for as much as three days. At the best of times Mrs. Brass had a tendency to sigh. She either complained or sighed. Gradually she was coming to sigh more than she complained. With her golden hair pulled back severely into a knot on the nape of her neck and her expression of a *Mater Dolorosa*, she had, in the most simplistic terms, an air of nobility. Franz Horn had a soft spot for this type of madonna. From earliest childhood. Still, he didn't really care for Mrs. Brass, which was why he made every effort to treat her in such a way that she would never get the idea that he didn't care for her. From others he learned that he was successful in this. Mrs. Brass let it be known everywhere that, since she had been transferred from Thiele to Horn, her faith in human goodness had been restored. Apparently she recited this formula frequently and vehemently in order that Thiele, the top boss, might hear about it and be annoyed. Because she had been a member of the staff since the founding of the firm and was considered a "personality," she could get away with this, and she knew it.

Mrs. Brass having finally left, Horn could once again turn his thoughts to Benedikt Stierle's terrible end. But already he could hear the cleaning woman invading the outer office. Unlike Mrs. Brass, she was not so easy to get rid of. Horn jumped up and, with barely a greeting, strode past the cleaning woman as if in a great hurry. His car was the last remaining one in the parking lot. Even Dr. Preissker's car, which until just recently had always been the first and the last, was gone.

Walking toward his car he saw that the round shiny object he had been noticing for the past few days was still lying on the ground. He walked over and picked it up but waited until he was in his car before examining it more closely. A ball caster. Probably from an office chair. After having ignored the ball caster for several days he felt justified in keeping it. His desk chair at home had casters like that. One never knows, his Vater Willi used to say when he picked something up. To Franz Horn's mind, even on a day of great disasters one should pick up oddments and save them.

Once seated in his car he wished he didn't have to

make any further movement. Here in his car he was safe from Mrs. Brass and the cleaning woman. But he was expected in Bodnegg. Hilde was already there. She had picked up the girls from two different trains; she had bought the gift for Horn's mother. His mother's name day was the most important family celebration of the year. All he had to do now was drive there. Thirteen kilometers.

But when, emerging from the industrial area, Franz Horn should have turned left up the Schussen valley toward the Allgäu, he turned right instead. Toward Spellmann-Strasse—i.e., toward home. He had left his sunglasses in the house. He couldn't expect Hilde to have remembered them too. In Bodnegg he needed sunglasses in June.

He parked the car in front of the garage door. In the mailbox there was a telegram: REGRET UNABLE ATTEND PARTY FOR AUNT KLOTHILDE ALL GOOD WISHES GOTTLIEB AND FAMILY. Franz Horn made a face. Not only were name days more important hereabouts than birthdays, but his mother's name day was of special significance. It was as if all the relatives wished to affirm their desire to make amends to this woman. Ever since his mother had been widowed, more and more relatives turned up annually on June 3, so that each name day became for his mother a feast of redress. But invariably this demonstration of affection for the widow also emphasized the fact that, while her husband was still alive, the family had tended to avoid her. This no longer bothered her, or, if it did, she didn't let on. She showed her gratitude to each person who came. She was genuinely happy to be one of the family again.

Franz Horn admitted to himself that, by failing to build the little house in Bodnegg for her until his step-father, Vater Willi, was dead, he had contributed to the condemnation of his mother's marriage. Wouldn't it have been simpler and cheaper to build it earlier on if Vater Willi, who had put up innumerable buildings during his lifetime, had lent a hand with the construction? But whenever Horn's mother said that in her opinion paying rent was a disgrace, Vater Willi had retorted: "Klothilde, you're nuts—I pay my rent, and that's all there is to it." The smallness of the apartment hadn't bothered his mother: what did annoy her, she used to say, was that the owner of the building always looked at her as if expecting her to say thank you, as if she owed him something. Her husband's response: "Klothilde, you're nuts." Apparently the owner looked at Vater Willi quite differently from the way he looked at her.

On the very day of Vater Willi's funeral, for which the relatives had turned up in surprisingly large numbers, discussion of the building project got under way. That evening the relatives had decided that their Bodnegg relative needed a place of her own. His mother had sat there passively enjoying the discussions. Franz Horn wouldn't hear of any of his relatives advising him on how to finance the project, that being something he was quite able to manage on his own. However, the lumber for the roof trusses would come from the family forest in Wigratsweiler, and Cousin Xaver would deliver it to the carpenter in his truck: this decision met with his ready acceptance. It was clear to everyone that only now, after Vater Willi's death, was it possible to start building. That was simply the way it was. Willi Horn, dyspeptic, a bricklayer, who smoked, drank, played cards on Saturdays and Sundays—the family had never expected a fellow like that to build himself a house.

Franz Horn had a guilty conscience whenever he thought of Vater Willi. Once, during a quarrel with his wife, Willi had shouted that the way her relatives treated him was worse than the way he'd been treated as a prisoner of war in Russia. Vater Willi—that was what, when the three of them were alone, Horn's mother had called the man who wasn't a father. Franz Horn had picked up the habit, but also only when nobody else was around. In later years he had tried out the abbreviation VW: Vater Willi had laughed at the little joke, so Franz Horn had stuck to the initials. Only after VW's death did Franz's mother tell him that he wasn't Vater Willi's son. From her manner of telling him he knew that was all she was prepared to say at the moment. She had told him no more since then.

Imagine Cousin Gottlieb having the nerve not to come to his Bodnegg aunt's name day! Yet he was always saying that Aunt Klothilde's name day was for him, the broker, the most important one, St. Klothilde being the patron saint of notaries and brokers. Surely he was aware of what that meant to his aunt, if he, of all people, stayed away, the only Ph.D. in the entire family! Contempt, that's what it amounted to! And there was nothing that Horn's mother was touchier about. Horn made up his mind to let Gottlieb feel his annoyance when next they talked on the phone, even if that didn't happen for weeks or months. Maybe like this: Hm, too bad you weren't there, my kids were really sorry—you know how fond they are of that dog of yours. That's exactly what he would say, those very words.

The sunglasses did not show up in the top right-hand drawer of his desk. But they couldn't be anywhere else. Franz Horn was meticulous. And glad of it. To go looking for mislaid objects was only for people with stronger nerves than his. He would rather be meticulous. By this time he had even become passionately meticulous. Keeping things tidy gave him satisfaction. He never tired of filing, putting away, storing things. Whenever he stored things away he thought of VW. In the little Bodnegg apartment and the partitioned space allotted to him in the attic and basement of the building, VW had stashed away incredible quantities of trivia. As a child, Franz Horn had had to help VW in this job. Over the years he had come to believe that he had pitied rather than admired VW for his obsession with order. Sheer pity had made him pretend to admire this talent. The only thing he had genuinely admired was that, while stashing things away, VW had never removed the cigarette from the right side of his mouth. No one had ever told Franz that his mother was living with VW in a Joseph's marriage, but he had always known, or rather, sensed it. There was no way of knowing. But to sense it was enough. VW wanted to make Franz a top-notch warehouseman. When Franz told his mother this, she called VW into the kitchen and sent Franz out of the room. Through the closed door he could hear her hissing at him. It sounded as if something were boiling away madly in much too small a pot. After that, VW had never again said that Franz must become a top-notch warehouseman.

One day Hilde had accused him, Franz Horn, of having a hoarding fixation, whereupon he had automatically quoted one of VW's pet phrases: "If it was up to you, everything would be thrown away." He discovered a VW trait in himself: he could never throw anything away. Pipes he no longer smoked, old rosaries, boxes that might someday come in handy, a slightly damaged Thermos flask, obsolete loudspeakers and record players, shoes not yet quite beyond wearing, intact parts of picture frames, children's beds, as well as patio umbrellas, motorized bikes, lamps, lawnmowers, temporarily unemployed locks, orphaned keys, parts of shelves, lampshades, unmatched screws and nuts, randomly acquired nails and tacks to be straightened at some point in a leisurely future, saddles from scrapped bicycles, intact parts of obsolete household appliances—there was nothing he couldn't find room for. He enjoyed keeping things. He now felt just as VW had felt: pride in always knowing exactly where to put his hand on something.

Hilde, on the other hand, threw everything away, saying she was afraid of suffocating if she didn't defend herself against his hoarding fixation. It was only after that nonsense with the pills, since they had been living together again, that Hilde had developed this aversion to what she called his hoarding fixation or, sometimes, his preservation mania. No doubt he had been meticulous in the old days, too. Perhaps this tendency had increased during the three years he had been separated from his family. Recently Hilde had been showing alarm at the power this passion exerted over him. To keep or to discard: this incompatibility was enough for either of them, if he or she were so inclined, to trigger the daily battle. When no battle was needed they could happily discuss the question of which had come first: his hoarding mania or her discarding addiction. In periods of calm, the fact that by this time one couldn't be imagined without the other was admitted by both. Then they would even admit that the discarding addiction and the hoarding fixation were interdependent. There was no more accurate way of expressing the interdependence on which their resuscitated marriage was based than by the dependence of her addiction on his mania and that of his mania on her addiction. But when the marital atmosphere became more charged again, there was no longer any consensus; then each would make ruthless use of the alleged mania or the similarly alleged addiction in order to unmask the other as the enemy he or she was.

If the sunglasses were not in the drawer, then Hilde must have remembered even them, too. Hilde remembered everything. She didn't point out that she remembered everything, and she didn't want him to point it out either. He could hardly pick up a piece of bread that had fallen off the table without pointing out that here he was once again caught up in the universal battle against sloppiness, dirt, disease, even death. He found it hard to do anything: Hilde found it easy. He hoped Hilde didn't compare her many activities with his own. Fortunately she had no way of knowing how little he did at the office. Whenever her energy got on his nerves, he could act the exhausted businessman. For some time now, she had been back in a full-time job at the school. There was also her singing, which was assuming an ever more important role in her life. With increasing frequency he found himself being congratulated on his wife by people of whom the last thing he would have expected was an interest in church concerts. But these days all churches seemed to have turned themselves into concert halls. During the years of separation from his family, Hilde had become a kind of celebrity hereabouts. It was only later that he came to realize who had picked him up from the hospital. He had that nonsense with the pills to thank for the fact that he was able once again to live with his family. If that was anything to be thankful for. But it was.

H E had been staring for quite a while at a photo that had lain in the drawer where the sunglasses should have been. A photo of Dr. Liszt. He pulled out the bottom drawer on the left side of the desk. This required some effort as the drawer was stuffed with papers and notebooks going back many years. That was where he consigned everything he couldn't endure for the moment but wanted at all costs to preserve for some moment in the future. As soon as one tried to pull out the drawer, the papers and notebooks seemed to rise up as if to prevent the pulling out because it was premature. This drawer was the right place for the Liszt photo.

In that picture, Liszt had removed his glasses and was holding them in his right hand; his arms were outspread. Since, furthermore, it looked as if he were about to straighten up after bowing to the photographer, the result was a gesture of invitation that was a parody of obsequiousness. Because in this photo Liszt's eyes were without their thick lenses, he looked defenseless, exposed. But also appealing. So unprotected. Franz Horn would have quite liked to hear Liszt's voice now. He wanted it to say something that somehow matched that inviting gesture of surrender. He could give Liszt a ring, of course. Liszt was living alone these days. The legendary twins were at boarding school in Salem. His wife was more or less living with a Polish woman who for the past few years had been hanging around the place teaching piano. Olga Steinmetz and Mrs. Liszt had become a couple about which nothing was known but everything could be surmised. Neither of them had learned in childhood what is considered proper behavior around here. They stuck out like sore thumbs from the prevailing local pattern. Although Dr. Liszt himself was anything but a native, when he did something conspicuous it looked unintentional. Until Olga Steinmetz came here to live, Mrs. Liszt hadn't been conspicuous either. She had always been that slightly impatient-seeming woman who painted those tiny pictures so full of details; only those who had become more closely acquainted with the Liszts suspected the discreet domination that she exerted over her husband, a domination he accepted as a permanent mark of distinction. Instructions given him by his wife in the presence of guests were accepted by him as tokens of tenderness, as if he wanted the guests to see how everything emanating from this woman made him happy. Liszt himself had probably been unaware of whatever had come to light since the piano teacher moved into town. Needless to say, if Mrs. Liszt hadn't been living here, Olga Steinmetz would have had to act the harmless piano teacher who, at most once a year and by way of a blatant Carnival costume, would give a hint of her hidden self. But since the two women did meet, they were bound to discover and betray one another. Now they were never seen apart. Liszt, whenever he joined them, seemed to be just tagging along. These days he seldom joined them. It was Mrs. Brass's contention that Mrs. Liszt had applied for a temporary injunction against her husband to prevent him from visiting his children at school in Salem.

Franz Horn could leave now. He wouldn't phone Liszt. There was nothing he would have rather done. But he couldn't. Not after that argument at the Halt-nau inn. The day after that quarrel, Horn had written Liszt a short letter. He wasn't interested, he had written, in whose fault it was this time; probably it was his own. For the first time he had to say he felt it had been his fault; so all right, why not him, Horn, for a change, seeing that in the past Liszt had started so many, if not all, of the rows they had had! Incidentally, he was sorry.

The day of their row had been Ascension Day, a week ago yesterday. A week ago today he had written the letter. No reaction from Liszt. No reaction at all! Incredible! The idea of phoning him now is grotesque. You should kick yourself for even thinking of it. For the first time it's your fault, in fact you admit it readily, you apologize—in all those years when he was to blame for the rows, he never, never, never apologized—and he doesn't accept your apology. Simply incredible. He's just humiliating you. Leaving you up in the air.

Franz Horn was glad he'd buried the picture in that bottom drawer. It really had been stupid to keep it for so long in a drawer he opened every day. What was he thinking of, looking at that man every day!

He wasn't going to call Liszt, the sunglasses weren't there, he could leave. He left. But halfway between front door and car he was overcome by weakness. He wasn't sure whether he could even make it to the car. He countered immediately: why *shouldn't* he make it to the car? There was nothing wrong with him! But wasn't his right knee giving way as if about to slide out from under all reliability? Yet if he didn't know whether he'd even make it to the car, he also couldn't know whether his strength would suffice to get him back to the front door. But by that time he had already turned around. Safely, as it were, he had reentered the house and reached his desk.

He sat there calmly; there was nothing the matter with him. That sensation of his knee suddenly losing all stability now seemed like a message from his body. That failure of his knee, a failure that had not been imaginary, had come to his aid. In the same way his body might have made use of a heart attack to enable him to turn back. Now he could tell himself there was nothing the matter with him. There was nothing the matter with him! Yet he was trembling. He was actually trembling. Something—this much he could admit to himself—had happened to him. Halfway between front door and car he had felt his self-confidence deserting him. He actually believed he had felt it deserting him, felt himself, as it abandoned him, becoming soft and heavy, craving for a collapse. And there had been a sound that he had felt rather than heard. A whistling sound rising with incredible speed to the point of inaudibility. At that moment his knee had offered itself. Now he was restored, he could walk again. Although the sensations he had had outside the house no longer prevailed, he knew exactly what it had been like. With the clarity of an extreme sensitivity to temperature, he had been aware of his insignificance. As clear as the taste of sugar or salt on the tongue: that was how he had experienced his insignificance. The extent of his ordinariness had been revealed to him in a kind of blinding flash. He didn't matter. He was trembling. Now that it was all over, he felt obliged to endorse the experience. Yes, yes, yes, he should be shouting! Acknowledge the truth of that blinding sensation of nothingness! Had he ever claimed anything else? Or had he? Not for a long time now! Really? In any case not now! Not at this moment! Probably everyone is equally insignificant, uninteresting, worthless. But even if that was so, he was only experiencing his own worthlessness. Everyone else, it seemed to him, was solid. Worthy. As for him, here and now, nothing could be more worthless.

But by this time he was over it, wasn't he? He really could walk. He approved of himself. What had happened to him was probably only the very last flare-up of some previous, long-since-phantomized ambition. A specter from a time when he hadn't yet approved of himself. He had long since become satisfied with himself. Satisfied with everything. Nobody could possibly be more satisfied. There was not the slightest danger, for instance, that he would ever again attempt some such pill nonsense. And surely that sense of worthlessness he had just had merely served to confirm this! After all, part of that feeling is that one is capable of nothing, let alone suicide. Now he even let pass this melodramatic word, which he normally avoided. So: he really will do everything possible to stay alive. But wasn't this incredible determination on the part of an utterly unimportant person to stay alive as long as possible—wasn't that an essential ingredient of his sense of worthlessness? Get up, man. Drive to Bodnegg. The family is waiting supper for you.

At that moment he knew it would be better to wait

for Hilde's phone call. He should have been up there hours ago. He could actually feel Hilde's will forcing him not to drive off before she had phoned to ask what was keeping him.

He pulled out that drawer again. Of all his desk drawers it was the fullest, the heaviest. He always had to kneel down to pull it open. He certainly couldn't tear up the photo. Throw it away? No. Outside into the fireplace on the terrace? Leave it in the bottom drawer. It will gradually slip down into the farthest corner at the bottom of the drawer; in the year 2090 a grandson will discover it, will look at the man with the defenseless, shortsighted eyes, will wonder why, in the last century, he held his glasses so far away from him, and won't be able to understand him. Horn had a sudden feeling that, with that gesture of surrender, Liszt was challenging him to hit out. Go ahead, he seemed to be saying, if that's what you want, go ahead and hit me! I can see you'd get a kick out of that! That's Liszt for you. That's Liszt all over. Wanting to be in the right. Liszt, the victim. Franz Horn, the perpetrator.

The phone rang. It was Hilde. What was keeping him? From her toneless, lifeless voice he could tell that his mother was in the room in which she was phoning. In his mother's presence Hilde was inclined to sound gravely ill. She positively faded away. A soprano voice that made every church nave vibrate, and now so faint, so languid! At one time his mother had resisted Hilde. Not only Hilde. But Hilde most fiercely because she realized that Hilde was the person against whom she could least prevail. Hilde had never quite overcome the self-restraint she had developed toward his mother.

He asked how they were, whether she had picked up Ruth and Amanda. They were all fine, she said, he was the only one missing. He heard himself answer that something had happened: would they mind if he arrived tomorrow morning instead of this evening? Benedikt Stierle had set fire to his plant, killed himself; this sudden elimination of their only competitor in southern Germany might give Thiele some ideas, and he, Franz, wanted to prepare a few notes that he could submit to Thiele on Tuesday. He was more familiar with Stierle's customers than anyone else. He had the feeling that Thiele would be expecting some suggestions from him to take care of the new situation. After all, they now had the field to themselves from here to Wiesbaden. Perhaps this was the right moment to review the present policy of no direct sales to dentists, only to distributors. Hilde might well be thinking that Thiele, now that he had sold fifty percent of his denture business to Bayer in Leverkusen, would no longer be interested in such propositions. Wrong, Hilde! Perhaps Thiele would now withdraw from the sale to Bayer! Stierle had thrown in the towel because Thiele was telling everyone he was about to sell to Bayer. "A merger with Bayer!" had been Thiele's melodramatic expression. That had been Stierle's death sentence. Stierle is dead. Why shouldn't Thiele now . . . oh well . . . maybe all that was a bit too fanciful. But he'd still like to work it all out, and early tomorrow morning, very early, with all this business behind him, drive up to Bodnegg. Hilde said: "That's too bad." Franz Horn thought: That's putting it mildly! Now he was determined to stay here. Had she seen his sunglasses? Yes, she'd brought them along because he'd left them behind. You did? Yes. Hm.

Message from his mother: he must be sure to arrive in time for breakfast. Hilde said now there'd be nothing for him to eat tonight. He sent his love to everyone and hung up.

He had made up his mind that, before turning to the new strategy that he wanted to work out for Thiele, he would call Liszt. He could ask Liszt's opinion on such a strategy memorandum. Then he could casually mention that he regretted that brief, wisecracking, inadequately formulated letter of his. He could see, he would say, that Liszt wanted the blame for that quarrel to be described in detail and acknowledged by Horn.

He realized he wasn't ready to call Liszt. Though he wanted to. He considered it urgently necessary. The longer one fails to deal with the consequences of such a quarrel, the more everything gets out of control. He *must* phone Liszt! Liszt must come out here. They would discuss the situation arising from Stierle's death. They would drink the local rosé! Liszt's favorite wine. Seven bottles. The precise number they had drunk in Haltnau. Horn could promise that there was no way he would become involved in an argument. He mustn't say that not even Liszt would manage to pick a quarrel with him today! That was exactly what would strike the wrong note.

Franz Horn reached for the telephone. But he

couldn't dial. In his mind's eye he saw Liszt, Preissker, and Ryynänen walking toward Thiele, reaching him, saw Mrs. Mutter going down on one knee. . . . He *must* phone, must say that the argument on Ascension Day, you know, that row we had out there in Haltnau, well. . . .

If he *did* call, that meant he would be taking the blame for the argument. He *was* to blame. But only in the way that Germany was to blame for World War I! After all, the other side had also known that our man at the wheel was drunk! Failure to avoid is also to cause! Even the most simpleminded motorist knows that to-day! Liszt, of course, knows so little about driving that it would be useless to offer him such a comparison. But World War I—surely he would understand that. On Ascension Day, Liszt had been freer than Horn. If he'd wanted to, he could have avoided the quarrel. The fact was, that fellow didn't want to avoid anything! To put it bluntly: Liszt had wanted Franz Horn to slither into a quarrel and be unable to extricate himself! But of course one can't afford to be blunt, not if one wants to live with other people. Yet it's better to be alone than continue a friendship that sullies everything! He couldn't possibly call Liszt now.

Franz Horn stood up and opened the window facing his desk. The Schussen valley had already sunk into violet cushions. He regretted not having driven out to Bodnegg. He must have believed himself capable of phoning Liszt, of inviting him here. He must have hoped to spend the evening with Liszt. Should he drive off now? He would be almost in time for supper. And why not write a second letter? A real letter in which he could present the facts calmly, in their proper sequence? He could admit to some things without having to admit everything. Must one admit everything? Would anyone do that? In a leisurely written letter he could ascribe to Liszt whatever historical share Liszt had in the crisis of their relationship or friendship. And all without reproach or flippancy. The main thing was finally to bring everything out into the open. To allow oneself to breathe again. Perhaps after clearing the air like that one really could build up the friendship on a slightly more formal footing. Until now, everything had seemed to be slithering away. Weren't they much more like enemies than friends?

Franz Horn brought up a bottle of rosé from the cellar. The first sip was enough to confirm once again that he didn't particularly care for this wine. It was only for Liszt's sake that he always kept a few bottles of it on hand.

He could start writing.

DEAR LORD LISZT:

Why do I call you that? The title presented itself as I picked up my pen. I am probably trying to convey a certain distance between us and at the same time recommend that neither of us takes this distance too seriously. Or should we? There is something lordly about you. You are always wearing that olive-colored suit with the leather buttons. No doubt you once chose that color because it goes so well with your reddish-blond hair. No: your wife suggested that shade of olive, right? For her sake you have submitted to that color and have remained mindlessly loyal to it. How many such suits do you own, anyway? I ask this question in the name of almost the entire company. Miss Hölzel, my former secretary, once told me that every new employee asked this question within a maximum of four weeks. Some people think you are making a statement, and they would love to know what about! May I in future say that you do it out of deference to your wife?

Surely you must be fully aware of how odd it seems when you turn up for a yachting trip on a May 24 dressed in that heavy material! Naturally you were also carrying your black briefcase. How much would you have to be paid to leave that dreary leather at home? Since you also had it with you when we met last year in that Bavarian restaurant in Hamburg, I now know that you undertake a day trip on Lake Constance and a week-long trip to North Germany with the identical briefcase. With the same gray-blue shirt. With the same purple bow tie. Or is it a joke of a tie? Well then, I believe I'm entitled to call you "Lord."

Needless to say, on that Ascension Day I scrounged together everything I could find to dress up as a yachtsman, which I am no more than you are. When you came toward me at the station, I thought: Thiele won't allow him on board in those shoes. One need only observe how Thiele takes care of his mahogany deck to forfeit any idea of stepping onto Thiele's *Chemnitz III* wearing such dreary clodhoppers.

But, come to think of it, how pleasant it was to approach Lake Constance with you through the dandelion meadows!

You told Thiele that the quarrel had been staged by me. When precisely, may I ask? When we were looking out the rattling train window feeling as if we were back in the nineteenth century? When we transferred in Friedrichshafen to the bus for Hagnau? Myself contentedly following your lead because I know your fondness for organizing. I admit I couldn't suppress the thought that it would never occur to anyone seeing us that we were bound for the same objective. But that didn't separate me from you. On the contrary. I did my best to convey solidarity with your appearance, one that struck an odd note on Ascension Day hereabouts.

We reached the Haltnau inn at one twenty-five. You can't say I didn't admire you for ordering a table for one thirty! Otherwise we would have had to sit indoors. The place was teeming with yachting types. It was I who suggested the meal: filets of lake perch in beer batter, accompanied by a bottle of rosé. You promptly agreed, although you did reject my suggestion of beer to quench the glorious midday thirst we owed to our walk from Hagnau to Haltnau: you wanted your wine right away. You lowered your head and looked at me over the top of your glasses with a half-comical, half-critical expression as if to say: Why, if I want my wine right now, after we've just been walking between those very vines, may I not have that wine? So: it was wine, right away.

We had only pleasant things to look forward to. Food and drink and, on the shimmering expanse of lake, the bustling idleness created by yachtsmen on a warm, sunny holiday. The breeze wavers between coming to life and dying away, so everyone rocks between lethargy and activity before succumbing to the agreeable torpor that is invariably induced by the combination of sun and water. Thiele would be tying up around three: we would have already seen him approaching and would be standing on the boat dock, two highly contrasting figures ready to go aboard and have a born yachtsman take us at least as far as Kressbronn, where he, our captain, would invite us to a doubtless magnificent dinner and top off the outing by driving us home.

So that you won't think I am trying to pin something on you, let me say at once: I am writing (again) to apologize. I insulted you. At the risk of offending you, let me also admit right away that these days I am obliged to write more and more such letters of apology. Most of the people to whom I apologize for my *faux pas* don't bother to answer. Like you. So I don't write to them again. In your case I must write again. I have gone over our quarrel so often in my mind that I can now present it in a purified state. I must say that, while the quarrel was brewing and I noticed that we were once again stumbling into a quarrel, I was incapable of warding it off or even slowing it down. I failed to realize, of course, how frightful this quarrel was. In allowing it to mount, I hadn't the slightest inkling of how bad I would feel afterward for having caused it. It was only the next morning that I realized the harm I had done. Throughout the trip home I was in a state of detachment from myself. I kept myself at arm's length. All the next day I refused to acknowledge more than a faint inkling. I didn't want to know about it. I could hardly stand myself. I wrote you that flippant note. Then immediately I fled again from the facts.

Now, a week later, I am forced to admit: my attempt to escape failed. The quarrel with you echoes within me like a series of blows. Each blow simply affirms that I am now empty. I no longer have you. I shall never have you again. I shall never talk to you again. Polite phrases in the corridor, yes. But no more than that. I have really made a hash of things. It is as if I had killed you. As far as I'm concerned, I have killed you. As you see, I am now thinking only of myself. I am not even wondering about your feelings, whether you are also suffering as a result of our quarrel. If that were so, you would have answered my note.

To be able to bear it, I am now looking at everything in the wrong light. After all, I know you can't answer. Not that facetious note. Although, mind you, you could have reacted to the note. It contained a total confession of guilt. Unconditional. . . . The note was a blank check. You could have entered the amount, the penalty, the punishment. For God's sake, enter something! But that's how it is: you won't budge. You're in the right—why should you budge? You're the one who was insulted. There is no greater happiness for you than being in the right. You have been offended. To the extent to which I am in the wrong, you are in the right. No matter what you're offered, you're not going to be bought off that position so easily. Once and for all, you're the one who was insulted. Your wrath is irrevocable. You are now beyond the reach of the guilty person. Let him crawl forever. And be ashamed. Forever. All of it forever.

So what did I say during our quarrel? I remember a few things: you remember them all. Even the little I do remember is enough to make me feel that you must insist on a permanent rift. Was ever anyone as blameless as you? Was ever so blameless a person reviled as much as you were by me? No. So you (through me) are the acme of innocence, of moral beauty. After all, in the days when things were going so fantastically well for you and so lousily for me, you didn't make fun of me in front of others. When you were right at the top, you didn't make jokes about me, who was then right at the bottom. No, I was the one who did all that, following a sudden but at the same time uncontrollable urge. But why did I do it? At one point during our quarrel I said that the most extraordinary thing about you was that you never misjudge the measure of what you can inflict on another person— you, the realist who is always in the right. You attack only someone who deserves it. You act against a person only when your superiority—not through might but through right—is inarguable. You act, as it were, never in your own name and interest but always for the sake of a higher cause. And you have a fine sense of the particular inferiority, the personal inadequacy, of your victim. At least, you always did in my case. You saw through me. You know my weak points better than I do myself. So those were the ones you worked on. . . .

Here I go, trying once again to wangle a right for myself. I would like so much to confess *why* I unleashed that torrent of hatred on Ascension Day. But I don't know why. I can only confess that you are innocent. Of that. You have probably never done me any harm. And suddenly I lash out at you and accuse you of inflicting the worst damage you could on me without running the slightest risk. Why? Tell me, please: why do I make such monstrous claims? And all that during an outing in May that seemed destined to yield a succession of lovely idylls. If you continue to keep silent and abandon me to the riddle of this unfortunate affair, I shall regard it as an act of meanness justifying everything I did to you! Good night.

Yours,
Franz Horn

FRANZ HORN breathed heavily and for a time continued to breathe more heavily than the occasion warranted: after all, he hadn't run up a mountain. Evidently he aimed to see himself as a tragic figure. Finally he simply stood up, replenished his supply with another bottle of rosé from the cellar, lit a cigar, and smoked and drank and watched the young moon trying to push off from the Allgäu mountains and leap into the sky. With no sense of the passage of time, Horn saw that the moon had suddenly made it and was now racing through the sky.

He searched for an envelope for the pages he had written, then pulled out that bottom drawer on the left. He had to look at the Liszt photo.

Even while reaching for the drawer, he knew it would be better to ignore the photo, but he couldn't help himself; he had to do the very thing he found most distasteful: look at that Dr. Liszt. And the time spent looking at him represented a kind of victory of Liszt's over him. He looked at Liszt. Impossible to imagine that at this moment Liszt would be sitting at home looking at Horn. Impossible to imagine what Liszt did at home anyway. What was Dr. Liszt doing at this very moment? Phone him! Out of the question. Set fire to the picture with his cigar to save having to go on looking at it. Before reaching the point of being able to burn the picture, he put it back in the drawer and went off to the cellar for a third bottle of rosé. There was something he had to add to his letter to Lord Liszt. Something that was beyond dispute. The historical dimension, so to speak. He removed the written pages from the envelope. There was some space left under his signature.

P.S.

Try to remember, please, our last quarrel but one! The one in Hamburg in March of last year. Also in a restaurant. But underground. At least six feet. We were drinking a Franconian wine. And it was incontrovertibly you who started it. Try to remember, please! You asked me for my watch and told the waitress to open the lid of the garbage can. She stepped on the pedal, the lid sprang open, you threw my watch into the can. From about ten feet away. You wanted to prove to me, you said, that you weren't drunk. The waitress reached into the garbage can, groped around in all the mess for my watch, found it, brought it back. Whose was it? You raised a finger. She gave it to you. Please open the lid, you said. The waitress laughed.

I admit that, earlier on, while you had been telling me in excessive detail what we would be doing the next day, I had been listening with half an ear to that waitress. She had been telling a customer about a ruined vacation: driven all the way to the Mediterranean, she and her husband, the rubber dinghy defective, one compartment not airtight, the husband cursing for three weeks about the rubber dinghy, then back to Hamburg. She was laughing all the way through her tale. Obviously she hadn't minded one bit that they hadn't been able to use the rubber dinghy. I admired that waitress. She had a little too much of everything. Possibly, though, I do tend to read certain things into a waitress because my mother had been a waitress.

At one point I tried to draw your attention to the waitress. Gesturing toward her, I said: "Too much isn't too much." But you never caught on and continued to hold forth about Hamburg's tourist attractions, oblivious to the attraction right in front of your nose.

After fishing the watch out of the garbage can with splendid indifference and handing it to you with a laugh, that wonderful woman was told to open the lid again. That was more than I could take. I hurried over to the can, stepped on the pedal, the lid sprang open, you threw, and once again accurately. That's what's so amazing about you: when you're drunk you succeed in whatever you undertake. I was thinking: Let's hope Hilde doesn't turn up at this moment. You remember: Hilde had taken Amanda and Ruth to a matinée at the theater, where *The Prince of Homburg* was being performed. Hilde is convinced that she must constantly provide the girls with something they can look back on in later years. It was a glorious Sunday. The copper roofs of Hamburg were glistening as if covered with green snow. And there was a breeze that seemed to accentuate the colors. The next day Hilde would be taking the girls to Kiel because Amanda wanted to register at the Ellen Kleve School for training as a calisthenics teacher. The school authorities must see, said Hilde, that there was someone standing behind the child, then they would treat the child quite differently. So we had the Monday to ourselves, for Hamburg or the island of Juist or North Germany. We would be eating spring flounder; you had already taken care of that.

When Hilde and the two girls came back from the theater, you and I hadn't quarreled yet. You had twice thrown my watch into the garbage can, you had acknowledged the applause in the restaurant, and this time the waitress had returned the watch to me. Later I discovered that the big hand had been broken off. Now we were all eating. Northern Bavarian specialties. You went to endless trouble to make us all happy. It was a shame, you said, that here we were in Hamburg eating northern Bavarian food, but Franz had chosen this restaurant because it was near the theater and he was afraid Hilde might otherwise not find us.

"There now, Mrs. Horn, that's what he thinks of your resourcefulness!" you cried as you raised your glass to Hilde. You behaved like a universal patron saint. Without you, we clumsy South Germans were bound to be swallowed up by the great northern metropolis. To draw the silent girls into the conversation you asked about the performance. Amanda looked at Ruth. Ruth looked at Amanda. But Amanda was looking at Ruth, so Ruth said: "Fantastic." And blushed. "Well then," you went on, "if it was fantastic we'd like to hear a little more about it." At that point I should have said: Why ask? Just look at them! (I never have the courage to say what should be said.) For Hilde and the girls looked as if they had just been feeling very hot. Flushed cheeks, shining eyes. As if they'd been through the wringer. Tragic, too. They were most decidedly not yet ready for our company. Something had churned them up, overloaded them. They needed time to digest it.

I can't say you got much out of those three. There had been potatoes lying all over the floor, they said: not just a few, but masses of potatoes. And masses of people, too, with bandages, blood-soaked ones. And it had been dark. And, in the dark, all those potatoes and injured people. "O.K.!" you cried. "But what about the plot? Surely there must have been a plot, too!" Amanda looked at Ruth, Ruth said: "Misunderstandings." "O.K., that's a subject," you cried. "God knows it is!" Since the arrival of those three, your voice had become so loud that it would have been ridiculous for any customer in the restaurant to pretend he wasn't listening to us, or rather, to you. Hilde took the girls back to the hotel. By the time she returned we were already quarreling.

In Hamburg you wanted to prove to me that it was easy for us to get along together there. That led directly to the quarrel. I had had my doubts about this plan right from the beginning, my lord. It's easy to get along together in Ravensburg, too! And anyway: nobody asked me! Maybe there were such things as unsettled accounts, Mr. Liszt! Oh, indeed there were! And yet you expected paradise to begin right then and there. I knew only too well why. You had just had a chance to see a side of Mr. Thiele that only those see whose usefulness to him is beginning to decline. I know all about that, my lord: how Thiele looks at one the way a bank manager looks at a customer for whom he has just had to put in a reserve in his balance sheet. And your wife had just recently made her first few trips to Paris with Olga Steinmetz. For months Mr. Thiele had been shaking his head over you, just as he did at one time over me. He always does find out more than one would imagine possible. He knows how much we drink. He knows before we do when we become alcoholics. Needless to say, he was the first to know that your wife and that Polish woman were strolling along the Paris boulevards with blacks, and that the blacks wore purple trousers and patent-leather shoes with silver heels and silk jackets and inconceivably floppy hats.

Dr. Liszt drinks, one heard at the time. Such news leaves me cold. I don't shake my head. It's true I felt sorry for you, but before I would comfort you we would have to discuss that "unfinished business" on the agenda. What I mean is: I resisted the temptation to comfort you. You were in a bad way, I know that. You wanted peace with me. You were on the point of repeating those words with which you had so embarrassed me. Remember? In my apartment on Galgenhalde when Thiele left very quickly and you told me to my face that I was the only friend you had? But from 1971 up to that March Sunday in Hamburg you had assessed me for seven years in a way that I would never assess a friend. Always in terms of business. Always my qualifications! You were always objective in those assessments. Striving to appear incorruptible. "My Cato," Thiele used to call you in those days. He was proud of you. He could ask you whatever he liked, and you always told him what you considered to be the truth. What you said was never colored by personal considerations. You became famous for your objectivity. You created a veritable style out of your objectivity. A manner and a mania! Or how else would you describe it, Lord Liszt?

I presume you enjoyed that fame and that role, although I did gain the impression that you omitted to tell Mr. Thiele what you told *me* about Mr. Thiele. That he was a moneygrubber, and what you thought of his wife Annemarie. Through you, "Madame Annemarie" has become a cliché. Everyone knows that. Except Arthur and Annemarie Thiele. And, of course, young Master Johannes. Not that I'm reproaching you, my lord! Whatever one thinks about a person can be told to everybody except that person. He wouldn't understand. He has to be told what he wants people to say about him. That's all he understands. No one knows that better than I: it is Law Number One of our social physics. But then, is it permissible to watch oneself being stylized as the Great Incorruptible One? Shouldn't the lover of truth be the very person to do all in his power to be taken for a scoundrel? And is there any one among us who is considered less of a scoundrel than Dr. Liszt? In this respect, too, you seem to me quite lordly. . . . Here I am again, courting my own downfall with my desire to be in the right. Then there'd be no stopping me. Forgive me, please!

Before I come to our Ascension Day quarrel, let me state that I was certainly touched by your desire to make me feel at home in the magnificent city of Hamburg, to introduce me to your very special North. You were almost bursting with suggestions—to an extent that was quite alarming in a person of your size. Your throwing my watch into the garbage can was, so to speak, meant to express affection. You wanted to demonstrate, in one generous and sentimental gesture, that the affection you were then showing me came from a man who was master of his senses. It was beautiful the way you tossed my watch through the air with such perfect aim. But before we fell into each other's arms, weeping tears of fellow feeling, I had to settle those few points that must be settled if we don't want to lurch from one quarrel to the next. Believe me, I still have the feeling that at the time I was trying to build a house on soil that was regularly plagued by earthquakes.

Do you know what I was looking for in March of last year in Hamburg? I wanted you to admit that, with Thiele having brought the Austro-Finn from Helsinki, you were at exactly the same point as I had been when Thiele had brought you from Hamburg. I wanted you to admit, in Hamburg, that now, at the age of not quite forty, you too, through young Ryynänen, were becoming a kind of middle-aged uncle, as I had through you. Of course, I was already forty-four when you arrived. But you weren't even forty when Thiele brought along Rudolf Ryynänen. I left my family when you came. Your family, so it seems, is now leaving you. In Hamburg you made a show of friendliness, but you never said a word about the Austro-Finn. You couldn't. That's how he dominated you. Probably you took your fall harder than I took mine. You were younger than I had been, your self-confidence was far greater than mine had been. You regarded yourself, I believe, as irreplaceable. And then Thiele brings along an Austro-Finn with hair popping out wherever you look. Don't you agree that he should try to subdue his tangle of coppery undergrowth? But he does the opposite. He keeps leaving one more shirt button undone, chooses shorter and shorter sleeves, so that the hairy tangle forces its way out in more and more places. One can sometimes feel really sorry for that child's face with its bushy growth on all sides. I rejoiced each time he showed up. Because of you. I admit that. I felt you had it coming to you. Ah, when our Rudolf calls himself an Austro-Finn as casually as if he were saying the date: how about that! And what is your Hamburg as against his Helsinki! A tawdry opera cape as against natural fur. It is absurd to play one city off against another. But what won't we do to score a point? The Austro-Finn scored his points more brazenly than you did, that I'll admit. Although he is only seven years younger than you, he told you to your face that he felt like calling you Uncle—there was something about you. . . .

Those are Thiele's rewards.

You too had already been to our distributors in the south harbor in Helsinki. I had been there quite often, yet Thiele goes there just once and promptly brings back Ryynänen. And with him the surfboard production. That fellow has a patent dangling from every finger. In his family background he is not entirely unlike you in terms of the colors of adventure and the perfume of romance. In your case, it was the outriders of the Imperial Postal Service who, riding through the centuries, brought your family from Buda to Aurich,

where one of them, in order to render the name completely exotic, even had himself sent to the island of
Juist. But whereas in the telling of your saga you suffer
from a mania for accuracy that stifles all imagination,
the Austro-Finn tosses one gossamer-winged anecdote
after another into the circle of his listeners. How his
maternal grandmother came from south Tyrol via
Bosnia to central Finland where, while traveling by
train, she suddenly screamed because she thought she
had gone blind, but it was a tunnel, and she hadn't
known there were tunnels in a country that she had
believed to be totally flat! Do you remember? And
how about the experience of that grandmother's
brother in Bosnia when he saw the beautiful Jewess!
But Ryynänen says—thus promptly founding a club
of cliché connoisseurs: when he saw "his" beautiful
Jewess. And she saw him too, and he insisted that it
was Fate, and she agreed: in fact her husband, the
portly piano importer, also agreed, let him have her,
and fastened his last gaze not on his wife but on
Rudolf's great-uncle, saying: "Don't let me hear any
complaints."

One remembers things like that. Your accuracy
tends to obscure. You bring forward so many details,
all equally pertinent. I doubt whether you wish to in-
form. You want to tell a story. Preferably by nothing
more than your tone. And we are supposed to accept
your flow of words—gratuitously curbed to make it
sound more interesting—with the keen anticipation of
people whose lives are involved, although the only
thing that's involved is your craving to tell a story. In

this you are like a child who doesn't want to go to bed.
All right, so you feel compelled to regale us with your
origins. Perhaps, because I have nothing much in the
way of origins to brag about, I resent descendants who
boast of their ancestral tapestries. . . . No, it can't be
that. There's nothing finer than parading one's antecedents! I, having so few of them, am the very person
to appreciate antecedents. It must be due to your pre-
sentation, to the way you blow your own trumpet,
that makes me prefer to listen to the Austro-Finn, although he also has a lot to say about his ancestors.

Twice in your ancestral history you have reached the
period of Krems-Regensburg, twice I have forgotten
how the Liszts managed to get beyond Krems, and I
wouldn't put it past me to forget even a third one of
your orgies of accuracy. Am I being too hard on you?
Must one when in your presence keep off the subject of
the Austro-Finn just as you always do? This year the
surfboards are said to represent some twenty percent
of sales. Nine thousand boards! In the very first season!
What fuddy-duddy uncles we are, my lord! Neither of
us would have dared propose anything of that kind to
the company. For us, Chemnitz Dentures were an arti-
cle of faith regarded by us as definitive, even if we only
pretended to believe in it. You fought harder than anyone against that cheeky upstart. By that time I hadn't
much to lose. I went along with the idea right away
and arranged for the purchase of the land in Markdorf
through my cousin in Überlingen. I'm tired of trying
to slow down Thiele. Giving fifty percent of a well-
established company to a conglomerate and then in-

vesting the proceeds like that! A textbook case of high-risk diversification into *terra incognita*. But Thiele has the Midas touch.

So, if you had mentioned the Austro-Finn in Hamburg, if you had said: Franz Horn, I've come to that point too! We're in the same boat!, I would have melted. But simply to behave as if you were approaching me unscathed, as if you had decided at last to lift me up or admit me to your level. . . . No way! Not me! Hence my reserve. Which, of course, proceeded to irritate you to the point where you had to become aggressive. But in a manner in which only a defeated person is aggressive.

I was able to look on quite calmly in Hamburg. Without becoming involved. You resented that. That's why you had to sweep the wineglasses off the table and, when the sound of breaking glass had stopped, say, in a vicious whisper: "Clear the decks!"

My purpose in recalling this is not to shift the blame; all I mean to say is: in Hamburg I was not to blame for our quarrel, at the Haltnau inn I was, solely. Mind you, you could have tried to keep out of it. As I did in Hamburg. But you chose to become involved. More than I did in Hamburg. Or didn't you? But let's forget about Hamburg.

So. We sat down. From our table we could keep an eye on the boat dock where Thiele would be tying up between three and three-thirty. We sat facing each other, the way we will never be sitting again. I saw to that in the few hours that followed. You have told Thiele: "Franz suddenly went for me." According to you, without the slightest provocation I exploded in fierce hostility. Your thoughts had been elsewhere: suddenly my eruption, my fit of rage, my explosion, making the whole sequence of events appear planned.

I will try, since you refuse to do so, to lay bare the roots of the quarrel, my lord.

Sometimes, when I'm sitting across from you, I tend to recall how you treated me when I was still your rival, or—to be more accurate—you were still my rival. Your behavior toward me was never prompted by envy or fear of competition; there was no need for that, since I didn't represent a threat and was fifteen years older than you. Your motivation was purely a business one. The very thought of it makes everything in me contract, and a hard knot forms. There's nothing I can do about that knot.

People are now saying you're ill, that alcohol is ruining your health. Mr. Thiele is wallowing in sighs and insinuations. It's not an outright statement. I don't dare ask for fear he might infer some nonexistent note of satisfaction from my question. Besides, I don't believe that alcohol has any power over you. I can testify to your lack of susceptibility. The only reason you withdraw behind the veil of alcohol is so you can revel in your position of moral superiority without interference from Mr. Thiele and his company, without interference from any of us. I'll never be persuaded that you are not a voluptuary and, as such, a moral narcissist. You never tire of the feeling that *you* are in the right. I can see you grinning as you read this. You with your sense of humor. You have a great sense of humor. You consist almost entirely of a sense of humor. In your own case, especially, you won't allow anything to interfere with that sense of humor that coats everything with a blissful buzz. Particularly ever since your star—as Thiele would put it—has been somewhat on the wane. As far as your own feelings are concerned, you're still on top of the world, whereas I wish to point out to you what we now have in common. We must be frank about that. You must be made aware of the nature of the two men who were quarreling on that Ascension Day.

Do me a favor: give some thought as to whether Thiele talks to you on the phone differently these days from the way he did three years ago. His opinion of a person comes through over the phone. I take it for granted that by this time he treats you over the phone exactly as he does me. That's why I am pointing it out. When one has gone down in his estimation, he lapses, over the phone, into an impatient tone; from the very first word his voice acquires that hustling, relentlessly driving note. Automatically you feel you're a nuisance, a nuisance that has the impertinence to resist being shaken off. Have you noticed that tone, my lord?

Regardless of what you still wish to say to Thiele, or what he may have to reply to whatever you still want to say, that tone can convey nothing, absolutely nothing beyond the conviction that a phone conversation with you, or with me, no matter how short—and he sees to it that it *is* short—is too long.

I, a Thiele connoisseur, was aware of this tone long before I heard it applied to myself. Many were the times I experienced his optical-spatial variation in the plant, in the concert hall, on the tennis court: when someone who is not important to him involves him in conversation, he looks around, quite unabashedly, while the other person is still talking, then suddenly concentrates on someone whom he considers it more important to talk to, so that the one still talking to him has no choice but to accelerate his flow of words, like a tape, to double the speed. But all to no avail. Mr. Thiele walks away from him in the direction of the person with whom he has already taken up cordial eye-contact. You were always one of those who criticized such behavior as typical Thiele tactlessness and banished him to the outer reaches of good manners. The fact that Thiele is a man who is no good at lying, who must always do and say what he feels and thinks, has never occurred to you, Mr. Moral Judge. But that's the way he is: everything is up front and transformed into action. Probably only because he can afford it. But nobody mentions that. Yet the only thing to make one shake one's head might be the fact that a person can afford to be like that. And another thing: where would Thiele be today, where would the company be, hence where would *we* be, if he had allowed every conversation to ripple on to its natural conclusion?

Incidentally, the best way to find out how you rate with Thiele is to look at your watch when he phones you on New Year's Eve. When I tell you that there was a time when he phoned me at midnight, you'll say:

Pure fantasy! Meanwhile that has, I admit, become for me somewhat like a light that is still traveling from a source long since dead. These days Thiele calls me early on New Year's Eve, just before six. And wishes me a happy new year! Each year his call comes a little earlier. At the crucial time, during those chaotic minutes of the changing year, other people are now being favored. So why don't you check when it's your turn? Then you'll know.

Ah, my lord, how happy were those miles we walked from Hagnau toward Meersburg! Then we really were at peace! Please don't pretend now, with hindsight, that in anticipation of an attack from me you were walking beside me with your elbows defensively drawn in! Yet that's how you described it to the boss! Didn't our hike progress in a mood of delightful flippancy? You had brought along a map we didn't need, but you insisted we sit down on a bench, and I solemnly followed your finger as it traced the route. Did I agree? you asked. And it was purely a fun question, just as the map was a fun map, the day a day of fun, of pleasure, of spring, and so on. You decided—and what could have been nicer than your humorous way of surveying the terrain and then deciding—that, rather than walk along the lakeshore path, we should follow the one halfway up the slope, through the vineyards. The lakeshore path, you said, would be as crowded that day as the Jungfernstieg in Hamburg on a Friday afternoon. And how right you were! We had the path leading between apple trees and vines almost to ourselves and could look down on the crowds. You made us look down quite often. Each time I was only too happy to confirm the wisdom of your planning. Thus our walk turned into a delightful stroll through a madly burgeoning world. For a while the path led across meadows, and the hiker in his earthy, sturdy oak-tree getup skipped aside into the foaming blossom to pick some cuckooflower for the companion in lissome yachtsman's rig. About to stick the pale flowers through a buttonhole in the pseudo-yachtsman's faded-denim vest, he cried out: "Not enough contrast!," then pranced back onto the meadow to pick some mauvish-pink ragged robin with which to adorn the pseudo-yachtsman. The pale cuckooflower he planted in his own somber lapel.

Our mood was so playful that we were determined to take whatever came our way as an adventure. Do you remember how, before leaving the last of Hagnau behind us, we were fascinated by the sight of a man, who must have been all of seventy, chasing after his wife as she hurried toward the garden gate, and seeing him grab her just before she reached it—I mean, grab her right hand, that was all he was after, then snatch something from her, something that could only be a small key? An ignition key. He had the look of a man who has spent his life issuing commands. The well-tailored, creamy-white trousers, the navy-blue blazer with gilt buttons, proclaimed a man accustomed to reviewing the fleet. His face was purplish, distorted now with effort and rage. His hair was creamy-white like his trousers and carefully arranged to cover his scalp. I

really did think that for that little person not to throw
him the key immediately was heroic. He could have
made mincemeat of her without even trying. More by
psychic than by physical force.

As we walked on, we amused ourselves by invent-
ing a likely scenario. You maintained that the woman
was his daughter. "But she must be at least fifty!" I
exclaimed. "So what, my dear Franz? If he's seventy-
five?" you said. "But a fifty-year-old daughter, tricked
out the way she was, wouldn't let her father snatch the
car key away from her!" You said: "It's like this, my
dear Franz—her father told her: 'Go, by all means, but
not in those purple leather pants!'" I countered with:
"Those pants hadn't been purple but aubergine, and
not leather but satin, and most likely the retired admiral had already killed her by now. "In that case, my
dear fellow," you cried, "if he killed her it must have
been his wife!" And we agreed to look the next day in
the paper for a report on a crime of passion at the western end of Hagnau.

"My home!" you said, pointing to the vineyard turret at the end of our path. To me it sounded like "our
home." I know that's how you meant it. You didn't
intend to keep that square room forming the top half
of the turret to yourself. I know that. Half-timbered.
Windows on all four sides. There we stood, our imag-
inations at work. At just the right moment you
pointed to the Haltnau Vineyard Inn immediately below us, and beyond that across the narrowing lake,
explaining the treat you had prepared for us—for me,
in fact: the Widow Adelheid's "soul endowment" to

the hospital in Konstanz. That, you told me, was what this whole vineyard property had been. Naturally I smarted a bit at your knowledge. On the one hand I am touched by your boning up on such facts, but the way you trot them out implies that I should be ashamed of my ignorance. At the words *soul endowment* you look into my eyes with brute avidity. Only when I see from your avid expression that you are out to trap me—to trap the local boy into revealing that he doesn't know what a soul endowment is: only then do I lose that bit of freedom needed to admit this, and I manage to return your gaze as blandly as if I knew all about soul endowments, yet I can't help blushing. And you, sure now of your triumph, cry: "And what is a soul endowment, my friend? Well now, dear fellow, it is a donation whose proceeds are to be used to ameliorate the status of a deceased person in a worse Beyond, in other words, for the reading of masses." But then and there you delivered me from my minor dilemma by adding: "Fresh out of a book!" And went straight on to recount a legend about Wendelgard, daughter of the last Haltnau owner: a girl with a pig's head and afflicted with a hump. Meersburg wouldn't have her but Konstanz would and thus came into possession of Haltnau. So, you deduced, we were now stepping onto the soil of Konstanz and knew that, no matter how odd we looked, as long as we paid our way we would be welcome. "That's reassuring, wouldn't you say?" you remarked, looking at me. "Do we have pigs' heads?" I asked. "Who knows?" you replied, almost too seriously. I recalled your wife's telling me

long ago that you suffered from being ugly. At the
time I was too taken aback to be able to answer. Never
for a second have you seemed ugly to me! There's
nothing ugly about you! Today I wonder whether
your wife didn't persuade you that you were ugly so as
to dominate you with even greater ease.

As we walked down from the little turret to
Haltnau, our souls were in perfect harmony. The turret had united us in the wish not to have to live in these
disruptive times; yet with your Wendelgard tale you
had deprived the past of something of its charm. So
what else was there to do but take off into the land of
caprice? The vines all around us were showing us the
way.

I suppose we must have looked a bit like oxen deco-
rated for the Whitsun festival when we arrived at the
Vineyard Inn down by the lake.

It's scary—sorry, slang irritates you, so let's say: it's
dreadful—no, that's not what I mean, it's frightening,
you know . . . now I've got it, it's alarming to think of
all the things that can trigger a disaster.

Up to that point your behavior toward me had been
that of glad-to-be-of-service. That's how it seemed to
me. You played the role of someone who is anxious to
please and enjoys that role. You were even gentler than
you had been fifteen months before in Hamburg, and
that in turn irritated me. You were kindlier, more con-
fiding, than you had ever been before. Look at this
mighty fellow, I thought, watch him bowing and
bending in every direction! It seems as if this time you
were watching like a hawk to make sure you never

made any move I wouldn't approve of. You were making it very clear that this time you would avoid anything and everything that might lead to any kind of tension. That day I would never be given a chance to pick a quarrel with you. Such blanket forestalling did, I must say, rather get on my nerves.

Initial situation then, almost the same as in Hamburg, I thought. But on this occasion, in Haltnau, I was a different person. I wasn't about to set any conditions. I demanded no admissions. I no longer sought satisfaction. At last I was prepared to get along with you unconditionally. What's more, I felt capable of doing so.

So, united and happy, we arrived in Haltnau. Hot and thirsty. You with your fair complexion redder in the face than I was.

The place was full of yachting types. So I fitted in right away. Or rather, I looked as if I fitted in. If only you would tell me someday whether you mind not looking as if you belonged! Do you enjoy that, or aren't you even aware of it? We've known each other all these years, yet I still have to consider both as being equally possible. In other words, I hardly know you at all. That probably explains why I keep doing everything wrong. Can it be that that is the very thing you enjoy? Or how else would you describe it, Lord Liszt?

Apart from you, there was only one man there wearing a suit—the professor. Remember? I noticed him at once because he was wearing the kind of suit that until then I had seen only on our Austro-Finn: double-breasted, pale beige, almost colorless, reminiscent of recycled paper. The suit of our Rudolf tends a little more toward the lemon yellow and the trendy. That of the professor was colorlessness itself. And had never been anywhere near an iron. 100% natural. But presumably silk mohair. And as for his shirt! The finest of blue-and-white stripes, with a collar of wonderfully mild, pale blue. Seeing that shirt, I imagine it without the collar, and instantly all the men I had ever encountered between Wigratsweiler and Bodnegg in dark, slippery, acrid-smelling barns come marching past: they had all worn that shirt, without a collar. And now it serves to adorn the elite. That makes me feel proud, my lord; the absurdity of it is almost enough to make me sob.

The professor paid immediately for each glass as it was brought to him. He was concentrating on the boat dock even more than I was. Since I was also paying for our drinks as they came, he noticed that we were waiting, too.

The most beautiful thing there is the trees. The trees beside the water. The water reaching up to the trees. The meadows with trees and water. And then, of course, the steeply sloping vineyards. Everything else growing up the slopes. Right from the water. Let's not forget the wind. I'm not trying to soften you up. But trees, meadows, vines, water, plus wind—there was every reason for us to take it easy. Or were you indifferent to all that? Perhaps it was my fault that we didn't give Nature enough of a chance to affect us. In the back of my mind I was always hearing the exhortation: Don't shut out Nature! Remember where you are! But it didn't penetrate. We talked as if sitting in some plastic bar. Needless to say, we were discussing Thiele. We had finished lunch. I had crepes for dessert, you said all you wanted was the wine. I enjoyed the crepes so much that I threw discretion to the winds and promptly ordered some more. I admit that, as time goes by, my existential feeling consists more and more in having overeaten. I enjoy that. There is now nothing I find as agreeable as a somewhat overloaded stomach. It gives me a sense of detachment from the rest of mankind. And I find nothing wrong with that. What good would it do all those starving people out there if I were to eat less and yet do nothing for them? To shout yet again into the hideous face of unheeding capitalism that it. . . . No way. As long as the sole effect would be to salve my own conscience. Or how else would you describe it, Lord Liszt?

When I ordered the second portion of crepes, you raised your eyebrows high above the rims of your spectacles and exclaimed that obviously I had no confidence in Sir Arthur's galley. So it was you who brought up the subject of Thiele! In order to supply some common ground between us on this topic, and since you had spoken of his cuisine, I mentioned his digestion. It is exemplary. I wanted you to know that. Not that I wanted to score off you with my knowledge of Thiele's digestion: I merely wanted you to know— once every day and once every night he can void. Constipation is unknown to him. Smooth as silk. His own expression. Did I mention that? He's suspicious of people with gastric or intestinal problems. His experience: there's something wrong with them. Thiele—this is the sheer wonder about the man—is more asleep than awake when he goes to the john at night. This means his night's rest is not disturbed by that trip and the voiding. In those terms he has been able to retain the most exquisite state of infancy. It seems to me that, in this respect, he is more innocent than either you or I can ever imagine. I'd need to be put on the rack to admit to the humiliating procedures I must submit to if I'm to produce the bare minimum.

You did not regard my information on Thiele's digestive processes as an invitation for a meeting of minds. With Oho Franz! and Come, come, Franz! you acted amused indignation. How could I, you asked, know anything about your own defecation capabilities! And the next moment you were cockily maintaining that, compared to yourself, Sir Arthur (by this time you consistently referred to him as that) was a constipated owl. Only now do I realize that you weren't serious with your wild claims. You were being playful. You only wanted to bite my fur. I was supposed to bite back in the same way. Or, if possible, a tiny bit harder. All I felt was the provocation. That you wanted to score as some kind of Super-Thiele. Sir Arthur and Lord Liszt: bowel champions of the western world! In the other corner: Horn the martyr to constipation! Calmly and soberly I asked you whether, in the interest of the sanity of your/my position, it isn't mindless or simply meaningless for an employee to try to compete with the bowel movements of a boss, and his own boss at that. Surely that way madness lies! I cried. I felt hemmed in. Of course I should have said: By all means, that's O.K., you and Thiele, the great bowel champions! I should have said I had no serious intention of arguing with you about Thiele's digestion. If it is idiotic for an employee to want to compete with his boss in the matter of bowel movements, then it is doubly so for two employees to argue about which of them more nearly approaches the boss in that regard! But I was tongue-tied. You know how to play. I don't. You know how to toy, to retain a light touch even when scoring a point. Light as thistledown, as they say here.

Maybe I shouldn't have kept thinking that Thiele would be drifting up at any moment, that we should be prepared for the discussion he intended to have with us. I wanted us to be of one mind when he discussed the merger with Bayer. When Thiele invites us both to go sailing on Ascension Day, it means strategy. The subject was obvious: the move to Markdorf. The innermost circle is going to move. The rest will find themselves working for Bayer which, in practical terms, means for Dr. Preissker. Where do we fit in? That would have been our topic. But once you had posed as Thiele's bowel twin, I had no option but to quarrel with you. With this in mind, I implore you once again, with all the strength at my command: I beseech you to spare me any further reports on your own and Thiele's digestive processes! Is it such a luxury to wish for that? Have mercy! I can't ask Mr. Thiele for this. His urge to divulge is obedient only to his whim. But you can persuade him. You need only

tell him, in your subtly mocking tone, that indigestion-prone Franzl Horn had felt compelled to request
abstention from all discussion concerning defecation
and that he should be granted this aid to repression.

I merely wanted to remind you of the watershed: at
this point my attack on you, the surprised innocent,
began. At this point. You understand that! You do!
You do? Then please also try to understand what followed! Was bound to follow! This is the cry coming to
you through the night from your nevertheless conscience-stricken

Franzl Horn

ON C E again Franz Horn was breathing heavily, as if
he had just run up a mountain. This time, however, it
wasn't because he wanted to see himself in a certain
light: he really was out of breath. He had been writing
too fast. Now it seemed to him that for quite a while
he hadn't been breathing at all, at least not breathing
properly. After signing his name he had had to drop
his pen immediately, then he had shaken his hand and
wiggled his fingers to get rid of the cramp that went
from his fingers through his arm all the way up to the
back of his neck. He turned his head this way and that,
could hear the vertebrae crunching. It was some time
before he could breathe properly. After two glasses of
wine he felt ready again. He knew he mustn't stop
now. He couldn't dismiss Liszt like that. Not with
those insinuations. That had clarified nothing, settled
nothing. Hadn't even made amends for anything. Liszt

still knew nothing about him—Franz Horn. Just as little as he knew about Liszt. But now he had actually acknowledged knowing nothing about Liszt, whereas Liszt had never admitted to knowing nothing about Horn. On the contrary, in all his dealings with Horn he invariably acted as if he disposed over a fund of Horn knowledge that Horn himself would never even begin to approach. And how little Liszt knew Horn! This abysmal Horn ignorance of Liszt's must be put before him if he—Liszt—were to have at least some inkling of it.

Before he could resume writing, he had to look for the ball caster he had found in the parking lot, brought home, and put down on his desk. It had rolled off because Horn, with his vehement writing, had been jiggling his somewhat unsteady desk. Horn crawled around and finally found the caster under the radiator, but, on getting impatiently to his feet, he banged his head against the windowsill. He wanted to resume writing as quickly as possible. Lord Liszt and Sir Arthur would find out what manner of man their Franzl Horn was!

P.S. II

Franzl Horn—that's what you so often called me, my dear lord, when talking to Thiele. It was always kindly meant. In Hamburg they have a way of regarding everything that isn't from Hamburg as Bavarian. Okayokay. In the early days you used to pretend that for you Ravensburg was no more than a barely acceptable stop-off on your way to Brussels. You were thinking in terms of politics, weren't you? You wanted to protect your children from the local dialect the way the white man protects his stomach in Madras. One day when I told you at the Café Kraft that, in order to save the occasional item from Hilde's discarding mania, I intended to build on a *tuffet* to the garage, you laughed so hard that your huge torso began to quake. Never once have I managed to acquaint you with a local expression merely by using it. You forced me to translate. *Shed* and *hut* are good enough for you. The unmistakable and heartwarming capacity of a tuffet doesn't interest you. There is no way, for instance, that the word *tuffet* can imply a denigration of a building: that's the kind of word it is. You must excuse me. I was always trying to integrate you. Totally. How foolish of me. How wrong. How arrogant.

What's not available in English, you once said, isn't worth reading.

Now I've expressed what I wanted to say in the manner most likely to be misinterpreted. I'm no longer upset by trivialities. I'm too happy for that. I'm certainly happier now than you are. I'm not trying to score off you. I'm not being arrogant. I'm happy in the way people who have won a lottery are happy. You won't believe me when I say that I have no desire to move to Markdorf when Bayer—or, if you prefer, Dr. Preissker—takes over here in January. I had applied for a job with Benedikt Stierle! My letter went up in smoke with him. I know Thiele isn't going to take me along to Markdorf. I can understand that. You'll never understand why he won't take you along. Or do you actually still believe he will? But Markdorf—in other words, Fin Star—is already in production; apart from Thiele and Ryynänen, the Flipper Star Company needs no one from here. I'm glad to say I was never childish enough to consider myself indispensable. Thiele hates funerals—I quite like funerals, that's why, right from the start, he always sent me when the company had to be represented at a graveside. He'll send me to Stierle's funeral, too. Of all the functions I perform, Thiele probably considers my deputizing at gravesides the most important. He has a high regard for the fact that I do this for him and do it really well—and I do! All real-estate requirements have been met, and, what's more, the properties I acquired for him are large enough for a further three Thiele generations to expand on them. So much for that.

You still believe that you and Thiele have something in common. You haven't. That was what I was trying to explain to you in Haltnau. "There you go, my dear Franz, you're right back on the subject of those seniority problems," you said, and you called me an old hierarchist. You hoped it wasn't your fault that I could only divide the world like buttered toast into top and bottom. There must, you said, be some deeper reason. You advised me to see an analyst! Sir! Just because I was trying to convince you, by citing success and failure, that there's a difference between an entrepreneur and his employees! I believe you're still incapable of correctly assessing the objectivity of my (perhaps unfortunate) experience.

Maybe in the quiet of this night I will do better at making myself clear. I claim the following: the entrepreneur requires successes; failures must be borne by his staff. Failures must slide off the entrepreneur like water off a duck's back. He can function only when he's successful. Regardless of who actually performs that function, it is the boss who must receive all the credit. In the interests of all concerned. He must be able to believe in himself. We, if necessary, can get along without that. When Keith Heath went bankrupt in Coventry, *I* was to blame. When, during my last trip abroad, I salvaged London Dentures, it was at least as much Thiele's triumph as mine. And Thiele proceeded to give me credit for whatever share in that triumph seemed to him appropriate. Not that he begrudged us anything! As long as *he* is the person from whom we derive credit. And he can't afford to dole out too little credit: if he does, he can no longer have faith in us.

This shows how difficult the motivation formula is. Obviously there is far too little success in the world, so however much there is must be distributed with greater wisdom than anything else. For instance, I had to pretend to Thiele that the London Dentures agreement was conceived and implemented during the period following that nonsense with the pills. The truth is that I conceived the contract during the few days after the debacle in Coventry while I was hanging around indecisively in London. But Thiele was looking for evidence that, even after that nonsense with the pills, I was still capable of bringing something off. At the time I often saw him looking at me the way a housewife looks at a cracked pitcher. When the London Dentures agreement yielded its first fruits, Thiele invited me one day to his bungalow, which he hates so much. One can always tell right away with him why one has been invited. I knew it the moment he suddenly switched from our general chitchat to that deeper tone that positively vibrates with gravity and importance, a tone we all know.

"You drafted the agreement for London Dentures *after* that trouble of yours, right?" He always calls that nonsense with the pills my "trouble." Thiele had an avid interest in establishing that I had conceived the agreement *after* my trouble. He had been afraid that after that trouble I might have lost my drive. My reduced vocal capacity tells him that. So it must have been all right before. That's what I found out now. Relieved but still suspicious, he accepted my lie that the agreement had been conceived after the incident. What I heard in his question was: Please take pity on us—tell us that you drafted the agreement *after* your trouble! But if not, leave us and go, go wherever you like, we won't hinder you in any way!

Since that evening at Thiele's, I have known that he is capable of regretting his salvage operation. It goes without saying that he would do it again for anybody at any time, but, having done it, he can still regret it when he realizes how little use—from his point of view—I can make of that new lease on my life. Personnel, taxes, properties: he likes to call that "Horn's Sundries Department"; from his point of view that's

enough to fill a man. Sometimes when he looks at me I
see his eyes swimming with the darkest of dark-brown
pity, and I'm at a loss to explain that I neither deserve
nor require it. Spare me your pity, is what I should say
to him.

But you say: that's my delusion, my top-and-
bottom mania, the world as buttered toast—in short:
hierarchism! Very well, let's not argue about that. The
thermometer is to blame for the fever. Obviously.
And you've always had a genuine liking for Thiele,
free and easy, no inhibitions about rank, while I . . .
oh, my lord, when you were still his blue-eyed boy
you used to malign Thiele. Only now that you are on
the downgrade are you learning to love him. Who was
it called him a moneybags? How shocked I was at the
time! First I thought: Aha, you're so dumb, Franz, you
just don't notice who you're working for. Then I
thought: How can one say such a thing about a person
one's working for? Surely one must be able to respect
such a person, or what's the point of it all? One must
actually be able to like him! As I do. But you happened
to be the new star whose light was needed to give the
firm its luster. How foolish we looked, Mr. Thiele and
I, when you criticized us! On the other hand, we congratulated ourselves on having you. There were times
when Mr. Thiele actually reveled in your scorn, in the
severity of your judgment. Since you consistently refused to divide the world into this sphere and that, you
subjected each one of us to the most complete scrutiny.
The moment you heard something about Thiele's affairs with women, the entire man lost all value for you.

You rejected even that enormously hardworking, innovative boss merely because he couldn't pass a girl of the come-hither type without heaving an audible sigh in her direction.

To my surprise, I heard you talking quite differently about Thiele on Ascension Day. Now you have only praise for him. You are quite overcome with gentleness when you so much as say his name. And now you call him Arthur, or Sir Arthur. Now you speak of Thiele with a gentleness that is—if you'll forgive me—foreign to your nature. That makes me angry. I admit that. After all, in your eyes Mr. Thiele and I were rabble. Personally, I had the feeling you always regarded me as a kind of cheap radio with inferior tuning. Once, in Thiele's presence, you called me a twin of Georg Thomalla's. Remember? That's the kind of comedian you said I was! I retorted that I felt honored to be compared with Georg Thomalla. But then I said—again too loud—that you underestimated Thomalla, that you had no idea who he was, had probably never seen him either on film or on stage. "You're ridiculing someone you don't even know!" I shouted. And since all this happened before that nonsense with the pills, I still had both my vocal cords and could still shout. It was becoming obvious that you actually didn't know Thomalla. What a chance to tick you off! "Arrogance is rooted in your nature," I shouted. What I didn't say was: I, too, knew Thomalla more from hearsay than from personal observation. But since you were equating me with Thomalla, I had to defend him. How charmingly he plays men in drag! At that moment I was convinced of this. In my mind's eye I saw him wearing a smock and a kind of turban to protect his hair from the dust. "After all, a cleaning woman can't wash her hair every day!" I shouted, thus involving Thomalla and myself in a solidarity that wasn't going to be easy to shake. Thomalla as a cleaning woman in a print smock, with a kerchief wound around his head like a turban—there, what've you got to say now against that solemn, slightly sanctimonious face in all its womanly dignity! That trace of sanctimoniousness is meant—ironically!—to express naïveté. Raised eyebrows and pursed lips are his devices. Simple devices. "But I like them!" I shouted. "That's the difference between us, sir! The idea of the word *quality* being used to draw distinctions is abhorrent to me! I like quality!" I roared. "Everything has quality! There's nothing *but* quality!" I shouted and roared. "Especially where people are concerned! Nothing but geniuses! I *know* that!! I've seen it over and over again!! Up to now I've known nothing but surprises!"

I can still hear myself shouting. It's as comical as it's embarrassing. Phrases bellowed out like that into the night air are something I'll never forget. It's as if I had been hurting myself with those outbursts. Now that I have only one vocal cord I feel protected. That's one good result of that nonsense with the pills—I don't shout anymore. And now that I can't shout anymore, I no longer come out with phrases such as "Nothing but geniuses!" At first I thought it was the aftermath of a cold. But when my voice remained croaky, as you once called it, my ear-nose-and-throat specialist looked a bit farther down and reemerged with the words "recurrent paresis," augmenting that umbrella expression with "idiopathic, cryptogenic." I looked up the words at home and was embarrassed and grateful. My ENT specialist, an Apollo who for decades has been showing only the most superficial signs of aging and to whom I had not disclosed that nonsense with the pills, had turned my disorder into a kind of work of art, almost a case of art for art's sake, created out of nothing, nothing at all. Gradually it dawned on me that I was never to regain my full voice. So in Haltnau I didn't shout—that you must admit! But even without shouting I didn't manage to persuade you of the hierarchical nature of the prevailing structure. I am always the only person who sees it that way.

Oh, my lord, how I would like to draw you over to my side! Here's an example you must understand:

When Rosi Mutter, that aggressive personality, was still secretary to the manager of the Deutsche Bank, she revealed herself so unmistakably to Mr. Thiele one day on the tennis court that he hired her on the spot. Whereupon he sent Mrs. Brass down to me. Now known as Miss Brass, she was quite plainly being demoted. Since her sister, whom she hates, is still secretary to a manager, she found this unbearable at first. She would talk of nothing but her demotion. She positively demanded to be treated as a demoted employee. Now that she was a failure, she would say, nothing mattered to her anymore. It took her some time to acquire her present airs, which tend to resemble those of a deposed president-in-exile who is thirsting for redress. But at the time she was relegated to me, her sole attitude toward me was an orgy of submissiveness, whereas job applicants, male and female apprentices— in fact all those approaching her from below—were treated by her from the very first day with withering frostiness. So since that time I've been saying: "If one can endure an inferior, one can endure a superior." The second law of social physics, my lord. I didn't come into this world as a hierarchist. I never regarded Mr. Thiele as my superior. At first I was his right-hand man. He made use of me wherever he needed me. I preferred to work a hundred hours a week rather than ninety. Then he discovered you. From then on he realized that I'm not a person of stature but just small fry, a well-meaning bungler, our good old Franz, our Franzl. A thoroughly good soul. But no more than that. In self-defense I started to keep my distance. In-gratitude, they said! I became political. Thiele promptly dubbed me a Communist. I was lumped to-gether with Heinz Murg the foreman who, because he once forgot to add the antioxidant to the polymeriza-tion batch, was described as a "Communist saboteur." You must believe me: at the time I hadn't the faintest idea of where I was heading. I was groping. But Thiele and you knew at once.

Thiele became brutal. You became snide. You even seemed to enjoy the fact that I armed myself with an illusion which, for anyone still wishing to be consid-ered in his right mind, was nothing but an evil, stink-ing ruin. It seems that, in trying to convince myself, I merely betrayed my inadequacies. I abandoned my efforts. I groveled before your sweet reasonableness. I complied. Shed my burden. I wanted you and Thiele to have been and to be in the right. Now and forever. The instant effect: compliance alleviated the pressure of what had previously been unbearable. The hierarchy still in force in our company should by rights be embarrassing to us. But we are no longer aware of it. How fortunate! A person who complies gradually forgets that the only reason he no longer feels the pressure is because he has complied. Those who conform think of themselves as free. Like me, for example.

My father, who was a laborer, ended up having only one phrase: A racket, that's all it is! He didn't say everything was a racket, he said a racket was all it was. He allowed only one exception: card games. There you still found honesty. That was why from Saturday evening until Sunday night he spent more time at the tavern than at home.

You call me a hierarchist, my lord! *You* are the hierarchist! Because you have to be on top in order to live. I have a cousin who used to be his boss's chauffeur and was also demoted, transferred to the warehouse; after two months on the forklift he gave notice, bought a secondhand truck on credit, and now drives day and night for building contractors, paid by the hour, but he owns his means of production. He can think of himself as his own master. No Thiele can sigh at him every morning: "Things can't be that bad, Franz!" Thiele wants us to be cheerful. In the morning. It depresses him when we're not. He's so sensitive. Recently you've always been so ready to kid around; for

Thiele's sake, you want to cheer up all the others. You're so eager to please, all of a sudden. Oh, my lord, do you feel the water rising up to your chin?

A despiser of Thiele has turned into an admirer of Thiele. Right? That's what I wanted to hear from you on Ascension Day. As long as Thiele was flattering you, you and your high-minded, highly demanding wife were out-and-out Thiele despisers. When you were replaced by the Austro-Finn, you began to love Thiele. I can understand that. Thiele has shamed you. You called him a moneybags, he treats you like a gentleman. I have been watching your bittersweet superiority melt away, watching you having to admit what a fine fellow he really was, that Saxon fellow here in Upper Swabia. And now, in Haltnau, you were actually trying to talk me into believing that you had always loved Thiele more than I had. You made fun of me, with cold-blooded nonchalance you suddenly claimed that for the past two weeks you had been having breakfast every morning alone with Mrs. Thiele, and that you had been discussing the possibility of spending your summer vacation together—you and Mrs. Thiele!—at a castle in Austria because Mrs. Thiele wanted to take a course there in "metaphysical painting." With you! At a castle. Wearing not a shred of one's own clothing: nothing but robes of Indian cotton. No buttons, let alone zippers. Everything fastened with tapes.

Oh, my lord, that was the limit, that was nasty, nasty, supernasty. Or how else would you describe it, Lord Liszt? Referring to her as "Annemarie," the

woman who at one time was, for you, merely someone from the small town of Engen, an origin which, in
your eyes, although you'd never been there, merited
only forbearance—and now, a vacation with Mrs.
Thiele at a castle in Austria, metaphysical painting, Indian cotton. . . . And fourteen breakfasts in a row! All
this you hurled at me in the highest of spirits. As proof
of your consistently intimate relations with the House
of Thiele. At the moment you can find nothing in the
world more impressive than Mrs. Thiele's training in
that metaphysical painting. "I mean it, my dear
Franz," you exclaimed. "If you have eyes in your
head, you should have a look at those pictures." As if I
had been the one who had always referred to her as
"Annemarie"! As if you had to convert me! Not fanatically, though, or even seriously, but with that laugh!
However, you went on, if I insisted on remaining
blind to Mrs. Thiele, by all means, you wouldn't take
offense, relaxed person that you are, positively vibrating with unshakable, good-humored tolerance! And
familiar with every single one of the metaphysical pictures painted by Mrs. Thiele during the last two
weeks. Every morning you and she discussed her output of the previous day. And you convey to Franzl,
who is incapable of appreciating Mrs. Thiele, some inkling of the noble output flowing from the hand and
soul of that woman during those two weeks under Dr.
Liszt's supervision. Empty, formless backgrounds
with one color shading into another! All those pictures
had had that kind of hard-edged deliberate formless-
ness for a background. In the foreground, an angular

chair or a jutting ledge or a hard table or even steel. An object on which something else could be presented. For instance, two pears, side by side, and a third, lying apart. The third one, a mere slice of a pear. A naked slice. Peeled, exposed, the slice stands out beside the closed-up pears as they huddle, intact, together. And while you gaze interminably at that painting Mrs. Thiele says: "He peels me like a banana." She must have meant her husband, you had said. But she immediately forbids you to impute facile interpretations to her paintings. "My God!" she cries. "I refuse to lower the acme of metaphysical expressiveness that I have finally achieved to the level of This means That! There now!" she had exclaimed, radiant with a pride that was by this time far beyond the reach of any Arthur Thiele. That "There now!" was meant to induce the morning visitor, Dr. Liszt, to move on from the first painting to a second one: many delicate, naked, grayish-blue human forms, pressed together, seen from behind; but in place of heads they all have minutely painted snails or other shells. . . .

Naturally I could raise no objection to your gushing enthusiasm. Now that your wife is "into" painting—or was until Olga Steinmetz appeared on the scene!—what can only be called a "painting wife" is very much your territory. I grant that. But it so happens that I know for certain that, since early May, Mrs. Thiele has been on a Greek island. On Corfu, where she is in fact taking a course in that sort of soul-painting conducted by her Austrian instructor. So you, my lord, can only have enjoyed breakfast and discussions with Mrs.

Thiele during those two weeks in a highly metaphysical sense. That's precisely what I told you in Haltnau. This only made you insist all the more adamantly that for fourteen days in a row you had had breakfast with the painter and discussed her pictures with her. Now you were in deadly earnest. You looked at me . . . I can only say, menacingly! Your teeth clenched over your lower lip. That could mean only one thing: Either you believe what I say immediately, or . . . watch out! Enough is enough!! That's the way you looked.

But *I* knew, from several postcards received by Mrs. Brass from Corfu (all of them written and signed by Mrs. Thiele personally) that touched Mrs. Brass deeply, inspiring her to comment on the difference between Mr. Thiele and Mrs. Thiele and then between husbands and wives in general: *I* knew that Mrs. Thiele wouldn't be leaving Corfu before the beginning of June. But you wouldn't budge an inch from your inflexible and extravagant lie. Is that madness or is it not? It is not. The next moment you were already blithely skipping about again although I had just cut the ground from under your statements. You stopped insisting, you said in an airily affectionate, lightly tripping tone hardly to be expected of your six-foot-three oak-tree appearance: "Ah well, my dear Franz, in that case one of us must be mistaken, that's all! Since I am able to call upon the entrancing evidence of my own eyes while you merely quote scribbled postcards addressed to victims of impaired self-confidence, it seems to me that you haven't a leg to stand on. "But do we want," you went on in loud-mouthed gaiety, "to ruin our afternoon with trivialities? Can't we feel the exuberance of this pious day in our bones? Let's just ignore anything that fails to please us—what do you say?"

"Well, that's all right for you. But not for me. Unfortunately."

The next day I asked Thiele: "Where's your wife at present?" "On the island of Corfu." Thiele had already been fully informed by you about this controversy. I find that quite typical of you. Thiele said you had told him that, up to the point when I suddenly let fly at you, the two of us had just been fooling around. And because I had kept maintaining that you were spouting more and more arrant nonsense, you had as a joke resorted to the most outright nonsense of all: that you had shared fourteen breakfasts in a row with Mrs. Thiele during which you and she had discussed painting. But to take that seriously and get all uptight about it and insist fanatically on the truth: that was Franzl Horn all over! And so as to make me finally realize that all that random chatter was nothing but teasing and kidding, you had, you told Thiele, gone so far as to claim that you intended to spend a vacation with Mrs. Thiele in an Austrian castle! Good God, how thick does one have to lay it on before a Franzl Horn finally tumbles to the fact that he's being fed a cock-and-bull story! One really must say that, faced by such gullibility, there would soon be no fun left in telling fibs.

Also typical of you: disputing your lies is what you call gullibility. So I'm supposed to remember: when you get going like that I mustn't contradict you; you're allowed to say whatever you like, but if I challenge something I'm made to look like a fool because then you prove derisively that all your chatter wasn't really worth challenging. That's the way you want it, isn't it?

All right, I can see it now: I was bamboozled. Once again. The trouble is, you're constantly drunk. And when you're drunk you succeed in everything you do. You're then totally beyond reach, beyond accountability. You sail triumphantly over whatever hurdles of reality and common sense one tries to place in your path. Incidentally, I remarked in Haltnau that, no matter how much I drank with you, I could no longer get drunk in your company. The drunker you get, the more sober I become. The more of a loser. That's how it seemed to me in Haltnau. Now when I look back I must admit that I can't have been as sober as I thought I was. Maybe what happens is this: when I drink with you, the power of alcohol doesn't give me a lift or lend me wings, it weighs me down, depresses me. And everything one has trained oneself to endure then becomes unendurable again. Our private law: in your presence, alcohol affects me not as a release but as a disaster.

There's one point I cling to with a great sense of satisfaction: although Thiele has defeated us both, he defeated you more than me. I can tell that from the way you now praise him as extravagantly as you used to despise him. I still dare to say that he calculates the value of each and every one of us. Our value to him is precisely what we are worth to him. But to whom, may I ask, are we worth more? Our contribution is something he genuinely experiences. In fact, experiences most profoundly. And the beauty of it is that he manages to pass on this experience to each one of us! The radiance of his sense of satisfaction—one positively basks in it! And if each of us could bask by himself in the radiance of his satisfaction, everything would be fine. As it is, though, we have to compete for the spot upon which he lets his grace and favor shine.

The daily nine-A.M. session is intended solely to make us aware of how we are being rated that day so we can behave accordingly at our jobs. If he rates me cordially high, I must work all day in such a way that he will give me the same rating the next morning. If he treats one with patience, with forbearance, with conspicuous self-control, in other words with a doctor's bedside manner—he never scolds, for he knows he mustn't destroy our self-confidence—then we know where we stand and must try to catch up. In the final analysis we have to admit that, compared with him, we are numskulls. The fact is that, compared with him, we are short one motive.

He really is quite a rascal, that man from Saxony. If I were to tell him the day after tomorrow about the change of heart in the Liszt household, that pragmatic genius from Chemnitz would reply: If it's true that Liszt once despised me but now respects me, so much the better! And what a fool I'd look! And I wouldn't be able to put forward any business reason for making such remarks about you. Whereas you are objectivity personified, my lack of objectivity knows no bounds. The funny thing is that your terrible objectivity always turns out in your favor. Your advantage and that of the company seem to share an axiomatic identity.

At the time I didn't follow your rise with the same zeal with which you, for reasons of pure rationality, orchestrated my decline. Now you are declining too, may already be at a much lower level than I can ever reach. Mrs. Brass maintains that by now your job is being done by your secretary. You're drinking even in the office. I must admit: when Mrs. Brass whispered as much to me, I gained the impression that she was hinting at all she was doing for me. For she is protecting me as no one has ever protected me before. Minus her protection I would no longer be a viable member of the firm. I don't know what Thiele had in mind when he transferred Mrs. Brass down to me. Were two losers being thrown together? Or was I now being permitted to take over his secretary the way I used to take over his cars?

At first we hated one another. Then we gradually discovered how well we were suited. You see, I always fall asleep in the office. Because I never sleep through the night. When I wake up each morning between two and three, it is as if some restless, furious, nervous, greedy, high-strung individual in me had been waiting all that time for me to wake up. Have you finally woken up? he cries, and starts in immediately. There isn't a single problem he doesn't promptly bring to my notice, sharpen, ignite. Instantly I am wide awake, with no further chance of falling asleep again. Not before six or six-thirty. Just before it's time to get up I usually fall asleep again. Apparently to make it difficult for me to get up. And unfortunately that short sleep also erases everything I have been working out in my mind during those wakeful hours. All that remains is fatigue.

Result: in the office I fall asleep at the latest after an hour at my desk. But when I put aside my work to get ten or fifteen minutes' real sleep so as to be able to work again afterward, I lean back in my chair, feel the fatigue like pain, but can't sleep. Not until I try to resume working do I fall asleep again. It's obvious that without Mrs. Brass I would be finished. Just like you without Mrs. Zentgraf. If it's true—as I would so dearly like to believe—that you start drinking in the morning. An alcoholic! In that case, a fraction of the disgust aroused in Thiele by the Communist might well come your way. Farewell!

Yours sincerely,
Franzl Horn

P.S. III

Oh, my lord, just so I'm not guilty of causing a further misunderstanding: the rumor of your drinking in the office wasn't spread by Erna Zentgraf. How embarrassing if you were to believe that your secretary, who, as you know, comes to our house to take lessons

with Hilde, speaks badly of you here! Never! Your
Erna Zentgraf cannot but increase the world's sense of
pleasure. You are to be envied your secretary! Although, of course, the constant proximity of such un-
adulterated loving-kindness would probably drive me
up the wall. Every time she has to walk along a corridor in the office, she chooses to warble and sing. She
is permanently in the mood for singing. Practicing has
become second nature to her. That makes everything
easy. Hilde doesn't charge her for the lessons. Erna
Zentgraf with her plump cheeks, her high color, is
proof that goodness, too, exists in abundance. She is
enthusiastic about everyone. About you! About
Thiele! "They all spoil me so," she says. She doesn't
know what she's done to deserve it. Hilde says she
doesn't dare go on teaching Erna; she might even de-
velop into a coloratura soprano. So she has sent her to
Zürich, to Häfliger, for him to decide. Thiele, believe
it or not, has offered to pay for her lessons. And Erna
Zentgraf turns crimson when she tells Hilde that. She
has a bad conscience. Because people are so kind to
her.

Yes indeed, my lord, people hereabouts tend to be
modest. And there's nothing we like to boast about so
much as our modesty. And we love to point to K.E.,
our saintly meter reader who sang his way from the
humblest back alley straight up to the Holy Grail. So
please believe me: Erna Zentgraf, whom you may
have regarded merely as "buxom," doesn't gossip
about you. Gossip about you does exist and is captured
by Mrs. Brass's parabolic mirrors and then decoded by

her. But as for me, the sleeper, such drinking would only have brought you closer to my heart. It's too bad we failed to meet on that level.

F.H.

P.S. IV

There's one more thing you should know: how fortunate that you haven't answered my letter! Because of this good fortune I am asking you on no account to answer this letter either. When a letter is not answered it's as if a window that had only been letting in noise were to close by itself. When letters are answered they acquire an element of groveling, as if beseeching to be heard. If you were to answer I'd be afraid you might think I had written you in order to receive a reply. That would look almost as if I were dependent on your absolution, you being endowed with higher consecration: I always had a complex about that anyway. The Austro-Finn—thank God he turned up!—cured me of it. On my own I could never have cured myself of my sense of inferiority. Yet I had collected enough material to prove to you that you, too, are merely someone who serves his own interests at other people's expense. But with what embellishments! My notebooks are full of Liszt phrases. I am a collector. Thiele, the main character in my notebooks, advised me twenty years ago to keep notes on every customer. To avoid taking chocolates along to a diabetic or asking a homosexual to convey one's regards to his wife. Over a period of time I also kept notes on Thiele. With the best intentions. But eventually the notes automatically became a substitute for speaking up. I baptized my notebooks "Revenge Calendar." In the bottom left drawer of my desk I am hoarding these notes until the day of my retirement. Then I'll speak up. Somehow. I'll bring it all out into the open. I'm looking forward to that. At times I worry that, before that day comes, sheer decrepitude may cause the evaporation of the rage that prompted me to collect. Wouldn't that be a joke, my lord!

My Revenge Calendars are full, *so* full! Even the Austro-Finn has contributed. However, since he is more your adversary than mine, I might be of service to you. Generally speaking, though, the notes concern myself. They are often, I admit, minute details that I find it necessary to note down. For example: when you and I met for the first time—Thiele had invited us to the *Waldhorn* for some *loup de mer* and Sauterne—I wanted to show off with a book my wife had given me for my birthday. It was by Heinrich Böll. Ah yes, you said, the very same book had just been given to you too—not by your wife, though, but by her sister, who has a beauty salon in Castrop-Rauxel—you had dipped into it and promptly passed it on to your cleaning woman. That's how our first evening shows up in my Revenge Calendar.

There are two reasons why I have dubbed this collection of notes so dramatically: first so as to keep its purpose in mind, and second to remind myself that there might never be any more to it than its melodramatic title. Over and over again I panic at the thought that I might wake up one morning and feel reconciled. With exquisite neatness I enter every insult in shiny black, soft-cover notebooks with red edges. I would go out of my mind if I were suddenly to lose interest in retribution. At the moment there is no danger of such lack of interest. But tomorrow. . . ?

I must confess that things have begun to follow a typical course that I regard as a threat to my project. It goes something like this: Someone insults me; a solemn entering of the insult in the notebook, outline of necessary retribution, realization of present powerlessness, retribution postponed to a future, more favorable moment. One meets the insulting party again, even does him a small favor, that lulls him, enabling one to come down on him later all the harder. The insulting party is warmly grateful for the small favor, does me a small favor in return; we are generally regarded as being friends, the urge for retribution still exists but is no longer fresh—in fact it is now quite stale, it stinks.

That is the sequence I have to fear. Of course, by thinking up ever new tricks, you and Thiele see to it that, as far as you and he are concerned, I don't have to work that hard to keep my urge for retribution awake. There are nights when the lack of retribution would simply burn up my guts if I hadn't learned to postpone my most urgent need to some future time. To do this, I have to recite to myself reasons why I should not crave early retribution. No sooner do I recite these reasons than my fear returns that I might someday feel totally reconciled. Between the fear of perishing from lack of retribution and the fear of allowing that lack to die away forever because it is unbearable, I am tossed back and forth each night.

F.H.

P.S. V

Since you spend more time humming than thinking I must also tell you how greatly Thiele contributed to our Haltnau quarrel! He is not to blame. But if the *Chemnitz III* had turned up around three o'clock, I would have recognized her in good time by her exaggeratedly sharp, positively precocious bow and bowsprit. Since I had been paying for everything as we were served, we would, if Thiele had drifted up on time, been ready; we would have jumped on board and could easily have diverted our skirmish into a conversation rendered safe by Thiele's presence. I would have asked you to take off your shoes before stepping on board. Our arrival would have been comical enough as it was. I was getting jittery as it turned four, four-thirty, and far and wide no *Chemnitz III*. Dead calm, sure enough, but the *Chemnitz III* had an engine of at least 36 hp.

When I was called to the phone it was almost five. He had turned off to Romanshorn, where he was calling from, there was an absolute dead calm, not a chance of sailing, he was hoping that a thunderstorm this evening or tonight would give him a capful of wind to get him home. His regret sounded genuine. He cursed the doldrums. To use the engine from Romanshorn to where we were, and then from there to

Kressbronn: that would be an utter bore. He said. On returning to our table I felt miserable. For someone not to turn up renders him more precious than he really is.

Thiele had ditched us! O.K., so it was the dead calm. Fair enough. But Thiele's absence was Thiele's absence, and dead calm was dead calm, and one was simply not enough to explain the other. There are results for which their causes are inadequate.

Before the phone call you had just been regaling me with your fourteen breakfasts with Mrs. Thiele. I longed for Thiele to show up so I could ask him then and there whether you really had turned up fourteen times for breakfast with Mrs. Thiele. Now we would go on endlessly arguing about statements of this nature. I no longer felt any kind of match for you. Hadn't we sat down at the table as equals? Now you were so light and I was so heavy. Thiele could have provided a balance. Thiele was needed. In Thiele's presence we have never yet quarreled. Yes we did, once: when you tipped over the table in my house.

Anyway, I came back and reported the gist of his remarks, as casually as possible. "Well now, my dear Franz," you said. "You've landed us in a pretty pickle again." And you tried to persuade me that Thiele had merely been waiting for us to urge him to come here and pick us up without fail. Thiele, you said, was much more sensitive than people believed—especially than a Franz Horn believed who, being the rabid hierarchist he is, always tends to interpret sensitivity as diminishing from below upward. I might as well ad-

mit, you said, that I was an idealizer of the popular
soul! That's the kind of stuff you were shouting at me
across the table.

Fortunately there was no one apart from the professor listening to us. All the yachtsmen, kept here by
the absence of wind, were crowded around a table that
was much too small, making it seem as though, when
they were not on their boats that kept them apart, they
wanted to be as close together as possible. Without the
prolonged and slowly swelling din of voices from that
table, we couldn't have carried on our quarrel. I
couldn't have. That table saw to it that no one heard
us. Apart from the professor.

At the yachtsmen's table, some were speaking inces-
santly and simultaneously while all the others merely
listened and never contributed anything themselves. It
was as if a soup of noise were bubbling away in that
circle. The same bits and pieces kept bubbling to the
surface. The point at issue was whether one could see a
ray of light and not see a laser beam, or the other way
around. One man kept throwing the same question
into the discussion soup: Did all those around this table
believe that anyone could go to a land registry office
for information, or must one have special authoriza-
tion? But no one was disposed to argue with him over
this. In the end he had no choice but to join in the
laser/light-beam dispute.

Oh, my lord, how I envied those men! Why
couldn't *we* argue about laser and light! They were
blissfully happy. We were not. I had the impression
that the professor belonged more to our unblissful fac-

tion. But he didn't want to belong to us, oh no! Yet he was worse off than we were. For us there had been a phone call. The dead calm explained some things for us, nothing for him. When I turned to him and said there wouldn't be another yacht arriving here today, he replied curtly that he was being picked up by motorboat. I noticed that, as time went by, all he did was drink, forcing himself to look at the glass in his hands instead of at the boat dock. But from time to time he felt constrained to say something. Every now and again he would spew out a few words. And the moment he was aware of that, he was annoyed at himself. Then he would stare even more fixedly at his glass and compress his lips with even greater force. He wasn't going to let that happen again—speaking to us! And you never even noticed that he was a professor.

As soon as I had passed on the message from Romanshorn, the professor glanced up, beckoned the waitress, and told her that if a call came for Professor Eggteil it was for him, spelling out elaborately: Echo, Golf, Golf, Tango, Echo, India, Lima. So young, yet a professor. I flatter myself that I can always tell whether a person is accustomed to being looked at. I always noticed when a person is pampered. The professor was pampered. A face whose features not only were handsome: those features seemed to be fully aware of their effect, that face knew it was handsome. A full cap of hair, brassy in color, ending in the gentlest possible curve on the soft pale blue of his collar. He seemed to me to be battling with himself over whether to admit defeat or go on hoping that his friend would be along in the next five minutes. His face continued to win out over the assault waves from within, to fight for the expression that it knew made for the handsomest effect. Only the eyes were beyond his control. His eyes looked as if they were sweating.

I maintain that that young man, that professor, is to blame for our quarrel finishing up more acrimonious than ever. I could have done without that professor. If anything, I felt sorry for him. You rambled on at him just as vaguely and cheerfully as you did at me. "There's someone sitting at the next table who's fed up with everything," you said, without looking at the professor. "Come, my dear Franz and dearest Franzl, you as a valet to humanity will not fail . . . come now, what kind of a performance will you give us? Wedding at Canaan? That's right up your alley! But since by now we have everything that could be used in those days to impress—since by now we are quite obviously suffering from a surfeit, a surfeit so great that one among us is already bored to tears, and that on Ascension Day—Franz, what can we do? We can reach up into the trees we're sitting under, and, abracadabra, we transform common-or-garden Lake Constance leaves into a dainty little handkerchief and present it to the person who is bored to tears, at the same time introducing ourselves, quick as a wink: Allow me, my name's Veronica. . . ."

That's how you were talking. The professor was listening. You notice such things. I found it embarrassing. Annoying. Obviously I wasn't enough of an audience for you. I wanted to slow you down, steer

you back to our table. I shouted a bit at you. As for
you: "I must say, my dear Franz, since you've acquired
that croaky voice your name should be Crow not
Horn!" That's what your jokes were like. The professor chimed in a few times, and you each tried to
outdo the other in inanities. You were both drunk. I
wasn't. Not in that way. I deeply resented your establishing that inanity-twosome with him. Three times in
a row he said: "Fuck Donald Duck." Four times, as
quickly as you could, you said: "Suck up to Puck."
Whereupon you both laughed. Guffawed. And raised
your glasses and drank to each other.

But suddenly the professor regained hold of himself
and subsided into mutterings, clutching his glass with
both hands and glaring into the wine as if he wanted to
bring it to a boil. I saw a chance to get you back into
conversation with me. I was prepared not to hold
against you anything that had happened so far. When
Bayer takes us over in January! That's what I wanted
to discuss with you. It was time I confessed that I had
applied for a job at Benedikt Stierle's. I pointed out
that you still had a chance to advise Stierle not to take
me on, just as, many years before (purely from business motives and out of loyalty to the system and as a
matter of good judgment), you had advised the Co-
logne plant not to take me on. I pointed out that you
had once even advised Thiele against ever making me
head of Foreign Sales. I pointed out that, if Thiele had
ever offered me Foreign Sales, I would have refused. I
proved in detail how long I had been wanting to get
away from Sales. Sales means war, I croaked. I pointed

out that you had wrested Langer & Siep in Hamburg from me, saying afterward that it had been merely the result of a New Year's Eve joke; after a good deal of alcohol you had made a sentimental speech at Thiele's about Hamburg: that Hamburg was your true home, and the territory was being handled by someone to whom everything North German might as well be Eskimo—how could anyone have taken you seriously? Only Thiele, with business in mind even on New Year's Eve, had taken it one step farther and transferred Hamburg from my shoulders to yours. I pointed out how glad I had been that you had wrested Langer & Siep from me because I hadn't known how to cope with the young crew there. I described in detail my most recent experience with them: my phone call from the hotel to confirm the appointment set up by letter, the assistant manager's query—who was I? After twenty years! Twice every year I'd been there, had arranged the best possible terms for them. Then I pointed out that you had done me a real favor by gradually restricting me to home base. For years I had been finding every kilometer painful. Metal fatigue. I pointed out that unfortunately you had not done it as a favor to me. I didn't mind being deprived of Hamburg delicacies, but you should have discussed that with me before making speeches to Mr. Thiele that later you were obliged to claim were not to be taken seriously.

Naturally I realized that you didn't want to hear any of this at that particular moment. Time and place could not have been less suitable. But I couldn't stop myself.

At last it was my turn! And just because I was aware of how wrong it was to point all this out to you on Ascension Day in Haltnau, I tried by vehemence and adherence to detail to prove the truth, necessity, and urgency of what I was pointing out. But that only made it the more incongruous. I would have done better to reduce my experience to a single, concise formula: that friendship between employees of the same company is not possible. I offer you this fruit of my Haltnau experience, once more and fully perceived, as the third law of social physics that we have both been working on: friendship between rivals is not possible. Or simply: rivals are enemies. More simply still: rivalry equals enmity. Or how else would you describe it, Lord Liszt? And the fourth law, my lord, just so you are aware of the kind of fantasy trip you seem to me to be on: All human relationships between boss and dependents are illusory.

Thiele is trying so very hard. And that's precisely what betrays him. To me.

Starting in January—yes, this is what I wanted to discuss with you, only this!—we will be members of an outfit with eleven levels of management, starting with assistant deputy manager and rising via manager and managing director to chairman of the board. You and I will be assigned to a place somewhere on this ladder! I have been told about this structure by a cousin who works for a similar outfit. But I already know enough about Bayer from my purchasing days when I used to meet our raw-material suppliers. Somehow I always knew that one day we would be taken over by Bayer. I never spoke about it, but anyone could have figured it out.

Maximization is the moral law of the economy. And the true dictator. And it was inevitable that maximization should sweep us into that outfit. One thing is certain: there's not a cartel-investigation commission in the country that cares a damn about us. For purposes of maximization, we are a sitting duck. The McKinsey questionnaires that Bayer has been requiring us to fill out over the past few months tell us what a treasure we had in Thiele. Our hands will be reaching out for Thiele the moment we no longer have him. Walking along the corridors we will come upon smiling efficiency experts who will measure the length of our stride and check the antiskid quality of our shoe soles in relation to the floor covering. Today Erna Zentgraf twitters and trills her way past our office doors. Since the McKinsey consultant has been in the building she may, I fear, run into him. He would start a column on vocal practice in the corridors and conduct a poll on the degree of disturbance caused by a vocalist passing open office doors. Whereas Thiele has offered to pay for her singing lessons in Zürich! Although, mind you, only after advising her not to join the union. The thought of her marching along the corridors side by side with the shop steward and inciting unrest instead of warbling Mozart airs was too much for him.

One year after the completion of the merger I would like to ask you, if I may, whether you still see me as the hierarchist! One year after the merger, the "divisionalization" prescribed by McKinsey will have been implemented. Ask Preissker. Sir Arthur, you must admit, has put us in a pretty vulnerable position. Ask Preissker. Preissker has told the Bayer people that he considers a forty percent increase in sales possible without increasing the present level of staff, provided the following are implemented: "restructuring," development of "goal-oriented guidance resources," a "new controlling concept—vertical, horizontal, and functional." Thiele (according to Preissker) said that if he hadn't been working on the merger he would have initiated such steps long ago, hence the McKinsey consultant and the Bayer envoy are merely doing a long-overdue clean-up job in the company. I still find it difficult to convert the capabilities of fellow workers into McKinsey-questionnaire units while keeping them in the dark about it. Identify activities: Query forty percent of them! In other words, consider them unnecessary! The unfailing patience and courtesy of the McKinsey consultant remind me of the soothing sounds and gestures performed by the Bodnegg butcher as he tries to persuade our pig to stand calmly and without fear while he applies the stun gun.

How many "man years" have you amassed by totting up activities? I hadn't wanted to be around by the time McKinsey moves on to the second round and the queried forty percent must be translated into employees' names. But unfortunately Benedikt Stierle failed to play his part. The prospect of his competitor now producing everything from raw materials to finished dentures, in a single company, came as a shock to him.

He was an inventor, not an economist. In fact, people used to say that he didn't know the meaning of five marks. He would have been the right partner for me. I have a way with figures. Had it been he rather than Thiele who discovered me in the Internal Revenue Office and hired me away, he would still be alive, and so—if I may say so—would I. I am convinced of it.

Benedikt Stierle was a dreamer. He would have had to rely on me. It's fifteen years now since we first met at the trade fair and he said: "Too bad you're not in business with me." In those days, nothing existed for me but Thiele, i.e., Chemnitz Dentures. I laughed when Stierle said that. I wasn't even polite enough to pretend that I, too, regretted not being free to join him. I simply didn't take him seriously. That constant twitching around the eyes, those plump little hands— in those days such things were quite enough for me to put anyone beyond the pale. Oh, my lord, that was eight years before you appeared on the scene! I have you to thank for my having now to some small extent become aware of the worst instances of the callousness to which I'm inclined.

In the days when Thiele discovered me in the Internal Revenue Office and hired me away, a Mr. Bull was still employed in the company. He was then fifty-four, I was thirty-one—two years older than you were when you joined the company. This Mr. Bull was proud of being Thiele's right-hand man. At meetings he spoke so ponderously that to listen to him seemed beyond my powers of endurance. So quite often I would laugh. That made him insecure—something he hadn't been before. For four years I shook my head, grinned, laughed, and eventually my nickname for him, "Bullfrog," became established. He would puff himself up like a frog, his shiny round head was attached without neck to his round torso, his eyes bulged from both sides, and one could only wonder why he hadn't always been called Frog. The Bullfrog took early retirement when he was fifty-eight. Through me he had become nonviable. I believe I really was superior to him. I had nothing against him; it was just that I couldn't stand his way of organizing our work. And Thiele let me feel that I didn't need to control myself: on the contrary, for the firm it was in fact essential for this Bullfrog era to come to an end. I have the feeling that for years I concentrated on discovering ridiculous traits in Mr. Bull so as to prevent him from ever being taken seriously. Later it dawned on me that I was only doing what Thiele wanted. He wanted to get rid of the man. As a result he rewarded every silly joke about Mr. Bull with loud laughter.

When we went to the cafeteria, which we called the "chicken coop" because access to it was over a ramp with wooden slats nailed across it, we used to vie with each other in producing ever more ludicrous jokes about Mr. Bull. Mr. Bull never ate with us: he sat in his office eating the sandwiches packed for him by his wife. Thiele himself had declared that for Mr. Bull to eat in the cafeteria would be like committing adultery. Ah, we were quite a gang in those days! We all sat around two long tables in the chicken coop. At first Mrs. Thiele used to prepare our lunch with her own hands! She cooked creatively, my lord. Let her be proud of her "metaphysical painting"—*I* still look back with longing to her beef rouladen stuffed with bacon, onions, and parsley, and to her roast veal stuffing scintillating with herbs. To be able to arouse such longing is the ultimate.

In the new cafeteria the technicians sit at one table, the dental mechanics at another, the women polishers at yet another . . . and the food comes through a hatch and is not prepared here but delivered by a catering service.

I keep meaning to go and see Mr. Bull in his cottage in Salem. But I'm afraid that, when I enter, he will throw the nearest object at my head. I can't convince myself that he isn't still as resentful as when I last saw him. Before leaving the firm, he had written letters to the most important customers with veiled hints that Chemnitz Dentures was on its last legs and customers would do well to look for other suppliers. Miss Hölzel, the Bullfrog's secretary at the time, showed a carbon copy to Thiele, who immediately ordered Mr. Bull off the premises and sued for damages—a step he needn't have taken since the whole affair could be interpreted as a mental aberration on the part of a pitiable sufferer from acute resentment, a view to which even the press, both regional and national, gave full support. Not a single customer was taken in by the Bullfrog. The Bullfrog had failed cruelly. At a meeting of the entire staff, Thiele made a speech pouring scorn on the unsuccessful saboteur who, out of a sheer sense of personal injury, had unscrupulously jeopardized so many fine jobs. So the end result of this outrage was simply that everybody closed ranks around Thiele. And I was the hero who had always opposed this traitorous windbag. Thiele clasped me to his mighty bosom. Miss Hölzel was rewarded for raising the alarm by being appointed my secretary—yes, in those days that was still something of an honor.

If you hadn't turned up, I would doubtless have become a dyed-in-the-wool Mini-Thiele. So I owe you a debt of gratitude.

Although the big, the genuine Thieles may be justified on the grounds of being irreplaceable, the imitations that shoot up all around a genuine Thiele are not. Of course, if we could include the genuine Thieles in our present debate . . . but we can't. I can't. Therefore I must simply chime in with the everything-in-the-garden-is-lovely chorus. And everything *is* lovely. Otherwise it wouldn't be the way it is. Above all: it couldn't stay that way. Everyone is aware of what he's entitled to. Everyone realizes what he must realize: that he is entitled only to what he's entitled to. I must admit that at times everything still seems raw, abrupt, precipitous, intolerable, threatening, but that's simply because of the way I see things. In reality the pendulum has almost ceased to swing. As if everything were in perfect balance. Yes sir, without Thiele everything would collapse! Yes sir, Thiele keeps the whole thing going!

We two—the drinker and the sleeper—must thank

our lucky stars that Thiele is always enthusiastic. About everything. Those were the days when I could fancy that I only had to be against Thiele to have performed a good deed. Now he is delivering us up to the conglomerate. Serves us right. We didn't appreciate him. You didn't at all. I not enough.

For some time I have been worrying that he might lose his enthusiasm. On one occasion, some three years ago, I drew Thiele's attention to his extravagant life-style. I was referring to women. And I—not a superior type like, say, Lord Liszt—was concerned not with morality but merely with resources: after all, Thiele is the firm's source of strength. And squanders himself in so many beds. Wasn't it my duty to warn him? And in my interest! You should have seen him, heard his carefree laugh! Once again everything combined to form a total impression: his great tigerish teeth and, above them, those choirboy eyes. With that laugh he said: "It renews itself, Franz—you've no idea how it renews itself!" Did you hear that, my lord? It renews itself. Since then, whenever I see him gliding out of the factory parking lot in the aubergine shimmer of his car, I think: It renews itself.

It's really true that wherever he goes someone is waiting for him. Have you ever seen him slip into a parking space? No one else parks like that. Past the space and, before he is quite past it, he's already reversing and gliding swiftly in a single curve—drawn as if by the steel pen of a master hand—into the space that is always too short but precisely long enough for him. If at that very moment a woman happens to be standing at an upstairs window, she sees this, of course—and wouldn't that be enough to send shivers down her spine?

After he had assured me about that renewal, I was still left with the fear that he might one day be hit over the head with a poker. He does, after all, go into houses where there are open fireplaces, hence also pokers. Here's a fellow who for years has refused to board a plane, and he exposes himself to such danger! But although he can live without flying, he can't do without a constant parade of new girls. What I had regarded as squandering is in fact a source of energy. It's on account of all those new girls that he works with such terrifying energy. If he is looking for world hegemony, it is merely to have easier access to more and more new girls. Since knowing Thiele I have become convinced that a craving for girls is the motivation behind all aspirants to world hegemony.

Just so you don't think, in your moral narcissism, that I am trying to show Thiele in a bad light, I must quickly confess that I myself, though at longer and longer intervals, visit a woman with whom I used to satisfy my sexual needs while I was living apart from my family. We hadn't meant to become emotionally involved—Karin's husband, whom she had indulged, had left her for a Portuguese woman, a "guest worker" who was prepared to do even more for him than Karin was (competition everywhere!). But when I went back to my family and it was time for us to part, we found to our dismay that a relationship had grown up between us. Each of us felt pity for the other, and each, for the sake of the other, passed off that pity as love. To me, at any rate, it seemed cruel to stop visiting this woman simply because it was now even less necessary than before. Maybe I am overestimating myself. Maybe she would be glad if I stopped coming. She works as a waitress, and I go to see her, when I do go, only during her time off. But our relationship happens to be designed to such an extent for our mutual benefit that there is no room for truth and reality. I find it more and more difficult not to tell Hilde about it. I've now been back with the family for four years. Hilde trusts me completely: she couldn't imagine that I would ever "deceive" her. The extent of her trust defines the extent of my "deception." To the end of my life, or Karin's life, I will probably continue to drive to Eriskirch to see Karin, with slowly declining but never-quite-ceasing regularity and under more and more complicated conditions of secrecy. I will continue to sneak through the service entrance and then— up three flights of stairs!—perform a kind of strenuous labor which, if I were to be caught, would land me in unutterable disgrace.

The fact that for a while I deserted my family intrigued you at the time. And now you've been abandoned by your family! That puts you more than ever in the right where I'm concerned. Mind you, I'm not saying that you arrange things to enhance your immaculate luster, your righteous glow. It is simply that your immaculate luster shines forth with increasing brilliance. Everything that happens serves to polish your moral beauty, my lord. I admire you.

F.H.

P.S. VI

It is either recklessness or a fever. I am not myself, as you can see. Why, I am positively audacious! I find it amusing to turn my attention now to the Austro-Finn. A divine creature. Cheekbones almost as prominent as your wife's with her northeastern German background. Actually, he should appeal to you. But what I prize most about the Austro-Finn is his Adam's apple that bobs up and down like a sharp, triangular pebble between his little beard and the tangle of hair swirling up from his chest. It's time you understood: with Rudolf Ryynänen, Thiele can pursue a dream, and that dream has always been to build yachts. Once the Flipper Star Company has become Europe's biggest surfboard manufacturer, he may be able to afford his dream. His father started manufacturing teeth. Arthur Thiele would never have started with teeth. As long as I've known him I have felt that he wants to get away from teeth. For him the triple-layer tooth, as perfected as it has now become, is merely a matter of duty. I never took his compulsion seriously. His favorite animal is not the rat but the whale. The whale, my lord! Did you know that? To reproduce in boats the curves of the whale's body is the dream of this nautical person. Every year he donates ten thousand marks to Greenpeace. His way of fighting for the survival of the whale. I believe he sees the whales' plight as a threat to himself. For the last four years this totally agnostic man has refused to board a plane. He believes himself to be the victim of malice, perfidy, and chance and doesn't want to give malice, perfidy, or chance the slightest opening. You can tell to what extent Thiele is spellbound by Ryynänen from the fact that the Austro-Finn was obliged to use Thiele's means of transportation to travel from Helsinki to here: i.e., the ferry across the Baltic to Travemünde, whereas he doesn't mind *us* flying everywhere.

Rudolf Ryynänen! Thiele wasn't the least bit embarrassed to pronounce this name in our presence like a man in love. He was thrilled to the marrow. The railway station in Helsinki: the finest building in the world! Since his visit to Helsinki, he claims, he has come to understand—in fact, to love—art nouveau. Since that trip to Finland, he has come to hate his concrete bungalow. But his failure to give it up marks one of the overtones in his character, overtones for which, merely because they are not suspected, he is never blamed. Thiele saw the Finns as a people living under a single tree, and that tree is their language. So he said. They mumble their good-mornings like condolences, he said. Ah, Finland! In fact—ah, Scandinavia!

You must be pleased when he returns from his beloved Bergen and announces at the next meeting: Our real home is in the north. There they have preserved something that only our ancestors possessed here. We have lost it. Where else but in Norway's Bergen could he have found his ultimate authority on orthodontics? That had really impressed him: employing the growth power of the tooth in adjusting the alignment of the jaw! Combining the advantages of the American brace with those of the German plate! What the orthodontic authority in Bergen meant to Thiele in terms of teeth, the Austro-Finn now means to him in terms of floating objects. The choirboy expression in his eyes had never been as overwhelming as the first time he came back from Finland. It was as if he had been the very first to discover Finland. But that's how he is. Nothing exists until he discovers it, although I must admit that he discovers more than I do. Whenever he returns from some place where I have been too and then describes it, it is as if I had never been there. A language that doesn't distinguish between masculine and feminine words! Nothing, it seemed to me, was less likely to have thrilled an Arthur Thiele. But it did thrill him. In fact, he was full of Finland. You will recall, my lord, how he refused to wear anything but Marimekko sweaters, ties, and shirts. And raved about Luchti, a city where no one's allowed to wear red because communism is so hated there. That must have really swept him off his feet, for we know that, in his eyes, all evil originates in the Soviet Union. Look at what happened to Chemnitz, look at the Russian whaling fleets. . . .

Since, in moral terms, I am more stupid and thus a little less demanding than you, I have always loved Mr. Thiele more than you have. You now know that you can't afford to despise Mr. Thiele. Now you want to compete with me for him. At one time you were glad to let me have him, and good riddance.

But at first we sat there congenially, waiting for the

Chemnitz III to bring us our Tristan! One might say that Thiele spends all year in Bayreuth. I would feel embarrassed to listen to music like that in the presence of others. For each person, just by being there, admits quite openly that he is there only to listen to that music. I can no more go to Bayreuth than I can go to a porn movie. Anyone seeing me there would think: He must really need it! Quite true. That's why it mustn't be admitted. Thiele, on the other hand, goes to Bayreuth, sits tall and solemn right up front, and with every note imagines that he is Tristan. It's his music they're playing. He is the only one who counts. All the others are there for his benefit. Perhaps everyone in the audience is thinking the same thing, but, since nobody can admit as much to anyone else, everyone is free to go on thinking it.

Wouldn't you agree that our whole era is growing day by day more Thiele-like? His ability to believe in nothing but himself has meanwhile become the favorite virtue of our day and age. Thus, in his complete egocentrism, Thiele was way ahead of his time. But then he demanded more of himself than anyone I have ever known. For almost twenty years I—impressed as I was—allowed him to treat me as an inferior. I used to think: How is he to know that I am not inferior? He'll find out someday, I thought. It was only when you arrived on the scene and made me feel your superiority that I became touchy, suspicious, vengeful, and old, and day by day I am becoming more touchy, suspicious, vengeful, and old. I can't stand anyone over me unless I have put him there myself. I had conceded this position to Thiele. Temporarily. Never to you. For a while I believed in my own importance merely because I was convinced that Thiele needed me as the brake that he lacked. I implored him to invest more cautiously, to slow down production. I spent whole evenings trying to show him what would happen if everyone wanted to produce more than everybody else! Thiele says: "All you need is to be able to produce one day longer than the competition, and you've got it made!" In other words, world hegemony is the least one should strive for. I could foresee only disasters. Resources squandered, the earth reverting to a desert, but full instead of empty! Production as the annihilation of creation! That was what I was trying to show Thiele. Thiele was adamant. Fortunately! I was satisfied with not being responsible for this frantic consumption.

I have worked hard and conscientiously for my salary. I am the only employee—at least in this firm—to have requested a pay cut. Thiele granted my request. He will never be forgiven for that. The real-estate assets of the company, amounting at the moment to seventeen acres, are now worth closer to three million marks than two million. Haggled for and acquired lot by lot by me. With a capital expenditure of not much more than a hundred thousand marks. And just because I feel I ought to suggest it, he cuts my salary. Since then I have been working on my departure from the company. Benedikt Stierle—that would have been the answer. But even without Stierle I won't have any problem.

For a long time now I have been helping my Uncle Chrystostomus, not yet sixty and seriously ill, with the bookkeeping for one of the most thriving cattle dealers in the Allgäu. My uncle used to accompany the dealer on trips to Holland and Schleswig-Holstein. The dealer is also not yet sixty and also in very poor health. I could step in there at any time. Away from the world of plastics to that of cattle pure and simple. I shall leave before being made redundant by McKinsey.

That's what I wanted to tell you in Haltnau. By all means, pass it on to Thiele. I have lost all desire to tell him anything. I'm making you a gift of him. I hope you'll be happier with him than I was. Not for a moment must we stop indulging him! Come on now, admit it, admit to yourself that each one of us rehearses phrases and facial expressions before entering Thiele's presence. Yes, we are his apes. So much for that.

By this time I imagine you have already made friends with Thiele Junior. I admire the capabilities of that splendid youth. This Thiele III will go at a speed that will leave us all dizzy. As a student he founds a janitorial company calling itself Clean Sweep, equips a dozen Turkish "guest workers" with secondhand utensils, and, according to Thiele II, those Turks are now ready to lay down their lives for his son. That's how he finances his studies—as if he needed to! At the age of sixteen, during Carnival time, this Thiele III climbed through a toilet window into a dance hall, danced for two hours, and left through the official exit. There, saying he had mislaid his ticket during all that crazy dancing, he demanded a re-entry ticket so he could go back in after taking a breath of fresh air. Finally, he sold this re-entry ticket outside the premises for one mark fifty to some new arrival. As if he needed to! In four days he travels to Stockholm and back, for thirty marks including ferry ticket; in five days to Naples and back, for forty marks, but spends one day on a job that earns him a hundred marks. For nine hundred marks he buys an ancient Mercedes, drives it to Morocco, sells it there for three thousand marks, and thus has this trip, too, for better than nothing. As if he needed to! The fact is, he is a genius. By tinkering and careful driving, he reduces the fuel consumption of his VW from 6.9 to 6.7 to 6.3 liters per hundred kilometers.

And by now this genius in matters of thrift has acquired surfing trophies and titles from Acapulco, Ibiza, Hawaii. He has been on this surfing binge for years. And now the father is about to produce surfboards. And—want to bet?—if surfing should be deemed worthy of the Olympics (and it will), Fin Star will be right there. Maybe we will be allowed to cheer the magnificent six-foot-six figure of Thiele III as he stands on the awards dais.

How beautifully that all dovetails—fin and fin, father and son, world-sport evolution and family expansion! It radiates such harmony, oh my lord, that, for fear something might soon burst, I would prefer not to be around much longer. When the genius takes over Fin Star, Thiele will devote himself entirely to his nautical urge: in other words, the man from Saxony will at last circumnavigate the globe. From one girlie beach to the next. I know that this is his plan. We two won't be part of it, nor wish to be part of it. Water is not our element.

One day last summer, since it was too early for my rendezvous with Karin and I am interested in super-markets, I decided to have a look at the one off High-way B 3 1, just outside Eriskirch. As I finished parking, I saw Thieles II and III, in yachting outfits, walking across the sun-scorched parking lot toward the super-market and its banners flapping in the breeze. Suitable music wafted from all sides. I found myself unable to get out of my car: I was overwhelmed. I was stunned. Although it was a fine sight to see two such flourishing and, no doubt, happy men walking along in the sun-shine, it cast a black pall over me. I was not equal to that sight. Probably in self-defense, I thought there could be nothing more disgusting than a father and son walking in glorious weather toward a supermarket where they can buy whatever they like. How unjust of me, how stupid! Nobody can be more welcome than those two men at the place they're heading for. No-body can be more innocent! There can be no more har-monious meeting between our two divinities: supply and demand. I felt like clawing my face with my fin-gernails. I had to admit that I was now a misfit in this newly dawning world. In the absence of privation I would be lost. For affluence I lack the theology, so to speak. People who lack nothing paralyze me to the point of terror. I gave up my visit to the supermarket and drove out again onto Highway B 31. Toward my rendezvous.

You had no idea, of course, that, as we were strolling along toward Haltnau, I was thinking of suggesting we use first names. Somehow—so my thinking went—we would be in a better position with Thiele, toward Thiele, against Thiele, on the *Chemnitz III* if we were on more intimate terms. Now I'm glad that in Haltnau you started on your tirades before I had a chance to offer my suggestion. And since tonight I have already begun to reel off laws: here is no. 5—a man has friends as long as he doesn't wonder whether he has any.

So I have no friends. Not one. I admit it. And you, my lord? I might also consider myself a friend of Thiele's, you know. He has no problem with the word *friend*. Must be his Saxonian background. I wouldn't have minded at all being friends with both you and Thiele. Three people can be closer friends than two. Provided all three desire nothing but the enhancement of all relationships. But when one of the three is a boss, and the other two are his employees, then . . . see above. Shall I give you a list of Thiele's friends? All top people between Zürich, Munich, and Stuttgart. I always felt I was in a constant draft when I was with Thiele. And I can't stand drafts. Always dress warmly when you go to see your friend Thiele. Ah, my Lord Liszt, I am far more tolerant than you give me credit for! It no longer pains me to notice that you are more popular in the firm than I am. People find you more likable than me.

At each proof of your greater popularity I wince a little, lower the tip of my nose by one millimeter— that's enough. Immediately I am suffused by a feeling of truly gratifying solitude. Furthermore, the slight lowering of the head produces a feeling of strength in the neck muscles. What I'm trying to say is, I can then endure with perfect indifference the knowledge that I am less popular than you. In fact, I enjoy your popularity: it is proof that you are unhappier than I am. When I hear that you were seen sitting in the Café Kraft, slumped in your chair, that your wife came in with Olga and that you were led out, inconspicuously, by the two women—when someone tells me that whenever you show up these days you reek of wine, I invariably feel an urge to phone you and invite you to move in with me; but it has remained a controllable urge. Besides, I know you would take the first opportunity to run me down as usual. Yes, in the evening I would suit you fine, as an after-hours buddy and boozing companion, but during the day, in the firm: unrelieved severity. No thanks, my lord. I am not divisible. Don't forget that! In future you will have to work off your mania for being in the right on others. I am no longer available. I intend to keep my distance! I can feel it now as an element that will support me: distance! At last a support! At last, firmness! By means of distance! And even if it were an illusion! May the Lord God preserve it for me! At last, certainty! By means of distance. A guideline (to use your own language). Distance! That's all it takes. A single moment of not being found in your presence and Thiele's is beyond price. To be able to hope for another such moment, a source of strength. To die at such a moment, the ultimate.

Franz

P.S.VII

Please don't think I'm under the impression that everyone is conspiring against me! It's much more likely that a number of individuals—some of whom don't even know each other—are working quite independently against me. Concentrically, so to speak. So: keep your distance, Franz!

Your humble servant,
Franzl

P.S. VIII

Am I also imagining that I flinch whenever I see the Bayer envoy? Yet Dr. Preissker always smiles so defensively, giving the impression that his face objects to having to smile. Still, he demands of that face the very thing it is most reluctant to produce: a smile. So it becomes rather a forced smile. And everybody likes him. Everybody raves about him. Each person vies with the other in saying complimentary things about Dr. Preissker. Much fairer than Thiele—that's the general tenor. And works much harder! Imagine: works harder than Thiele! Just because his car is already in the parking lot when the staff arrive and still there when they leave for the day. Desk-bound diligence. Thiele's diligence is movement, mood, stubbornness, imagination. But Mrs. Brass says of Dr. Preissker: "One can't help liking him." I wish I were able to trust that smile. Hell, what's wrong with a mouth opening sideways instead of up and down! O.K., so you get a good view of his perfect molars. . . .

In our very first conversation he told me he was completely at my mercy, since, in view of the general unsuitability of the human being for the industrial work process, personnel problems invariably drove him to despair. And when I was at a loss for a reply he went on: "People couldn't be less suitable for the work we offer. To function in the workplace requires a daily deadening of sensibilities." I still said nothing. But I nodded. We sat facing each other in silence and, as time went on, without embarrassment. He had uttered three sentences, as stony as his sideways smile. At some point he stood up, saying he hoped I wouldn't get the wrong idea if he always sat at the chemists' table in the cafeteria. I shook my head vigorously. He added, somewhat shyly, that the fact was he felt at home with them. I performed the pantomime of total agreement. He was welcome to believe that he had completely won me over.

As we shook hands, he said we must soon get together outside business hours. As soon as his wife arrived and they had settled down, he would let me know, whereupon I promptly and warmly and eagerly said that, as long as he was on his own, I would be only too pleased to have him drop in at our place whenever he felt like it. I meant it, I said—he'd be doing us a great favor. I say these things in such a way that the other person can't help believing me. How

kind of me, he said, and promised to come soon. He
shook my hand. His hand, as you will have noticed, is
cold and powerful. He loves climbing mountains, he
says, so is happy to have been transferred to this part of
the world. He certainly didn't want to go to Brussels.
He disliked traveling at the best of times. In that he
resembled our formaldehyde. In reply to my raised
eyebrows, he explained that formaldehyde should, if
possible, never be transported. Whereupon I acknowledged my own kinship with formaldehyde.

Meanwhile he has been at our place three times. He
felt more comfortable with us than with anyone else,
he said. My behavior is always such as to ensure precisely this result. He has only kind, good things to say
about you and other people. In this respect he is already as adroit as Thiele. I always feel that Thiele,
when he does that, is trying to assure me that he
wouldn't tell others, either, what he really thinks
about me, but only whatever serves to improve company morale. What Dr. Preissker said about himself
was probably closer to the truth: that he was patholog-
ically vain, for example, which was why he had gone
in for mountain climbing. That he didn't believe his
character was strong enough yet to enable him to head
a concern of this kind. That he was thirty-seven. That
one of his two children was deaf in one ear. That it was
feared the other ear might be affected. He is also quick
to bring out a picture of that daughter. And one can
understand why. The little girl looks as if her charm
would suffice to redeem the world. On the other hand,
wouldn't it be just as terrible if a less beautiful child

were to become deaf? Strangely enough, it seemed quite plausible to me that one of his children might become deaf. I feel sorry. It shows in his face. Appalling.

I don't think anyone has as good a contact with the new overlord as I do. Without planning it, I have done everything to get on good terms with him. My instincts function: I am amazed. Even so, I flinch when I meet the Bayer envoy in the corridor or the courtyard.

Mrs. Brass, who sees only how well I get along with Dr. Preissker, has suggested that, the next time he spends an evening at our place, I propose that he and I switch to first names. She has never suggested that I propose anything of the kind to you. Since her main concern is with expanding her sphere of influence, this means that you are a back number, my lord. Someone who takes more than he contributes.

For Mrs. Brass, the merger era marks the dawning of the Golden Age. No more Thiele-type whims, no more favoritism, no more being ruled by mistresses, no more barbaric irrationality of cruel emotionalism. For her the merger means at last the beginning of a just constitution. And it becomes clear that she even considers injustice when applied across the board to be an improvement. When she speaks of the satisfaction she will derive from the merger, the tip of her nose turns quite white with eagerness and dedication.

Incidentally, when you see me in animated conversation with the Bayer envoy and you feel like laughing out loud, go right ahead. At one time I would also have laughed at such behavior. I am convinced that I shall be doing all those things I used to laugh at. If I could remember everything I used to laugh at, I would know everything I am going to do.

F.H.

P.S. IX

I can also tell you precisely why you are as much out of the running for Markdorf as I am, my lord! When you joined the firm seven years and ten months ago, Thiele acquired a hairpiece. Just before you joined us. But now Thiele wants only people around who don't know that he wears a hairpiece. You joined a firm in which everyone had been observing Thiele's hair maneuver. Someone must have pointed it out to you. You were just in time to be privy to the secret. You will remain here. Most certainly. I should have looked for an opportunity to tell Thiele how much more agreeable he has become since wearing a hairpiece.

Just as other people hang on a fatuous "you-know" to every second sentence, Thiele used, after every third or fourth sentence, to put his right hand into his left breast pocket, produce a long, fine comb, and run it swiftly over his inch-wide strip of carefully arranged hair. The comb swept from ear to ear and, before you knew it, it had vanished again. By the time we noticed this mannerism, it was too late. To tell him *then* that he had succumbed to an irritating mannerism would have been too risky. When he was still performing the movement more slowly, less frequently, and was running the comb almost meditatively over the strip of hair that didn't require it—that's when we should have told him. All of a sudden, it seemed, we noticed that this pulling out of the comb and running it over his hair and putting the comb away again had become a neurotic compulsion. There were plenty of people who never noticed this mannerism, though they saw Thiele every day. It all seemed to flow so inevitably. But once noticed, it set one's teeth on edge a hundred times. Ever since Thiele has been wearing the hairpiece, his right hand dips into his breast pocket much less often and much, much more slowly, and now the hand reappears with his unfailingly immaculate, folded handkerchief, presses it to his lips, and puts it away again. A hundred comb performances have been reduced to perhaps ten handkerchief displays. A genuine decimation of a mannerism.

Sometimes he still passes his bare hand over his head. But only we old-timers know what that means. So Thiele has improved through his use of a hairpiece. Above all, that solemn producing of the handkerchief endows this superpowerful man with a noble, almost consumptive quality. Naturally he didn't decide to wear a hairpiece merely to combat the mannerism arising from his loss of hair. Like many men of his vigorous life-style, he regarded loss of hair as something discreditable. Which it isn't. In my opinion. The hair of sensual men is not necessarily on their heads. But it would have been pointless to try and tell him so. I could see, as clearly as could be, how he was trying to get rid, one by one, of all those who were in the know. At the very least he wanted to be out of the sight of such people as Mrs. Brass, for one. I am convinced that the real motive behind selling the half-share to Bayer is his need to get rid of the last of the witnesses. And you are one of them.

Pure delusion, you will say. Perhaps, when dawn comes, I shall say so myself. But the fact is that daylight, reason, etc., have been pressed into service. Bought, bribed. Only delusion is incorruptible. For that very reason, delusion—that most loyal consequence of perception—has been declared incapable of perceiving. Splendid. Carry on. Good-bye.

Most insincerely,
Horn

P.S. X

Oh, my lord, I watched you. You're not a bit different from me. When the professor ceased to profit from your sounding-off and simply sat staring at the glass between his hands, you continued to hunch over our table, thrusting your head forward, although actually you were now talking solely for the professor's benefit. You were after him. Watching you, I understood why some people are said to be not exactly choosy about their methods. I leaned as far back as possible, keeping my eyes fixed on the lake: I wanted to make it quite clear to you that I no longer felt you were addressing me.

If only you had looked at the lake! It lay there as if everything were over. As if after a world disaster. Instead of water, molten lead. Already purple. Dead calm. The sight of a few motorboats still churning their way through it seemed quite incongruous. And

you happened to be saying—completely at random—
that everybody liked you, that you had no idea why,
that you couldn't help it—the simple fact was that everybody liked you, how could you possibly object to
that! Did I expect you to do your best to make people
*dis*like you—did I expect that? O.K., for my sake you
would do anything—O.K., for Franz Horn's sake you
would now have to pick a quarrel with everybody,
though by nature you were a person who only felt
comfortable in a state of peace, harmony, and affection, a person who had never quarreled with anybody,
quarreled—quarreled?—quarreled with someone?
Never. . . .

In my eyes you looked Egyptian. I mean it. Like
some animal god. Behind you, the light of the thunderstorm, a glitter combining every conceivable color.
As yellow as it was green, blue, or black. The result a
kind of fulminating gold. Outlined against it—you.
There you sat at our table, looking with your long
back like a crocodile. Exotic. Fascinating. Admirable.
Never would I be able to sit like that, talk like that.
And behind you the ever more poisonous thundery
light. It made one want to pray. On the far shore,
storm-warning lights were already whirling. The first
gusts scraped black scars on the surface of the lake as it
lay glistening like armor. And you were talking like a
madman. "Come now, my dear Franz, try to name a
single person I have ever quarreled with, name just
one, just to prove that I am deluded in my belief that I
live with all the world in a state of perfect peace. You
see, I don't even know what quarreling is, but *you*

know, Franz Horn, *you* will be able to name someone I managed to scrape up a quarrel with!"

I should have said: Your wife.

I did say: "Rudolf Ryynänen."

And you, quick as a flash: "*He* quarreled with *me,* not I with him." There was nothing left for me to say but: "Myself."

"Come now, my dear Franz," you cried, "you don't count! I didn't start a quarrel with you, we've lived in a permanent state of quarrel since Day One!" That's not true! I should have retorted. But I was beyond retorting. Besides, you were beyond wanting to listen. You wanted to talk. You started offering proof: that hardly had you arrived here when we'd driven together to Salem for lunch; that you'd turned on the car radio but I had promptly turned it off again, and that I had said: "In my car *I* decide when the radio is to be turned on," whereupon you exclaimed: "How is it possible to avoid living in a state of quarrel with such a person?"

With a power of recall known to me otherwise only among women, you proceeded to trot out details, but—so I maintain—in a purely arbitrary way. Like that turning on of the radio. I can't possibly have said that. So I maintain. But any further protest was useless. I did have one more try. "Just so that in future you can cite some real evidence of what separates us," I said, "let me remind you that three years ago you were in Milan with Thiele and returned six days earlier than he did. The day Thiele left I had handed him my letter of resignation. You came back, Thiele must have discussed my resignation with you, we saw each other every day in the office, lunched together at the same table: you made not the slightest reference to my letter of resignation. Let me tell you," I said, "I'll never forget that. Thiele had talked to you about me, no question about that. But you remained silent. That was quite a feat!"

"Come, come, Franz," you exclaimed. "How is a person to know that you approve of indiscretion!" That took care of what I had intended as a major reproach. It was impossible to embarrass you.

"You see, my dear sir," you went on, turning to the professor, "my friend Horn—who claims to know best just because he knows some things better than I do—claimed earlier today that you were a professor from one of the big cities of our republic. Well, I'm glad to hear this, because so far all my dealings with professors have been excellent. I was—if I say so myself—the favorite not only of my favorite professor but of all the professors I had anything to do with. But above all of Wieacker! Do you know Professor Wieacker? You mean to say you don't know Professor Wieacker, the great historian of jurisprudence? Ah well, you won't hear me reproaching you for that. Reproaches, you know, are the specialty of my friend Horn. Between you and me, Horn is the greatest living virtuoso in that field. If you should ever be looking for someone to reproach you, Franz Horn's your man. Since I exist on a knife edge with him, you can take it from me that I never exaggerate where he's concerned. . . ."

That's how you talked. It's true! The professor's reaction fell far short of your expectations. Now that even the motorboats had disappeared from the storm-tossed lake, he had given up all hope of being picked up. There had been no phone call for him. He looked at you even more morosely than he did at me. His hollow eyes looked like caverns of misery. He seemed —so I thought—to be begging you to stop talking. Every word you uttered seemed to cause him pain. His face winced under each of your resounding phrases like an oscillograph of suffering. All *you* noticed was that he was insufficiently amused by your performance. I could see how unhappy this relationship was. In an attempt to divert you from the professor and believing that the occasion now required some strong medicine, I asked after your wife and where she was. You raised your head and looked at me again, but the blue of your eyes seemed washed out, your gaze unfocused. We were on our seventh bottle of wine, and I had drunk scarcely more than one of them. Certainly less than two. You said: "Ah yes—tact, Mr. Horn, tact is a gift, isn't it? One can't expect to find it everywhere to the same degree."

At that moment a woman entered the restaurant from the Hagnau side, made straight for Professor Eggteil, said: "Viktor!," and tapped him on the shoulder. The professor looked up, jumped to his feet, swayed, and cried: "Gerhild! Gerhild!" He sounded as if he were about to burst into tears. The woman beckoned to the waitress and was told that the bill had already been paid, whereupon you cried: "Your eye-glasses, Mr. Horn, if you don't mind!" It sounded as if you wanted to have a closer look at the woman standing beside the professor. Your hand was held out so imperiously in front of my face that, incapable of the slightest hesitation, I gave you my glasses. You took them and, with a vicious jerk, snapped them apart in the middle and handed me back the two pieces. "Professor," you said, "as you see, I am doing my utmost to prevent Mr. Horn from staring immoderately at your visitor. I hope you appreciate it."

The professor's glance took in what had happened, but his expression had undergone a complete change. His face had regained its firm lines. His eyes looked at us as if we were dirt. But you were probably past noticing anything. I would have liked to send you a signal to have a closer look at that woman. The glossy aubergine purple of her satin trousers, the voluptuously swelling cream-colored blouse, the gold belt, the gold sandalettes, and now it was clear—clear to me, though I no longer had my glasses—that her lipstick was exactly the same shade as the trousers and just as glossy. Even her teeth bore traces of aubergine purple. But you were past seeing anything. You just stared. After having made fun of my staring! As far as the woman was concerned, we didn't exist. She had taken young Eggteil by the hand and was about to lead or drag him out when you shouted: "Just a moment, please, just a moment! The performance isn't over yet!" Whereupon you took your own glasses and snapped them in two, exactly as you had done with mine. You pushed the pieces toward me. "Friend Horn, the collector of eyeglasses!" you said. Apparently you were hoping to detain the professor and the woman by such displays of entertainment. But to no avail. The woman led the reluctant professor past us and out the door. But after passing our table he evidently remembered us again: he stopped, once more turned his handsome, newly firmed-up face toward us, and, in a tone oozing with contempt, said: "Hick comedians!" And with that he finally left.

You sprang to your feet and made what was intended to be a graceful bow, as if you had just been paid some wonderful compliment. I felt I'd made a fool of myself. In the eyes of the waitress. Luckily the yachtsmen's table could spare no ears for other customers. The subject of the land-registry office had subsided. Even the laser-beam/light-beam subject had petered out. Now they were arguing vociferously about the difference between conifers and coryphées, each man bent on explaining the difference to the others. Apparently each knew the difference but was convinced that none of his companions did. That's where I would have liked to be. That's where my kind of people were sitting. That's where my kind of topic was being discussed. That's where I belonged. What greater joy than to be sitting beside the lake with a May storm blowing up and, as part of an acoustic tangle, arguing to the point of exhaustion about the difference between conifers and coryphées!

"Momma's got him back," you said, after the woman had disappeared with the professor. From that remark it was obvious that you hadn't understood a thing. Later, on the way home, I did wonder why it had taken me so long to catch on that the professor was waiting for a woman. He hadn't been waiting the way one waits for a male friend. At least, not for a friend with whom one proceeds to have a long-drawn, knock-out fight merely for the sake of proving oneself to be in the right.

"Taxi!" you shouted.

That's when I had the only smart idea of the whole day. "One for me, too!" I shouted. I believe that found its mark. You felt hurt. For the first time that day you showed some reaction. You turned away theatrically and hid your face in the crook of your arm. Although you were acting as if hurt, you genuinely were hurt. No further word was spoken between us. I said good-bye to the waitress, who was busy rescuing the table-cloths from the gusts of wind. I apologized for the trouble I'd caused by paying so frequently. I had an impression that she was looking at me angrily. "Did I do something wrong?" I asked. "I hate this job," she answered. I turned away from the sullen waitress and followed you out onto the road leading to Meersburg. We stood there without speaking. I thought you might have more to say: after all, you had seemed to be in stride. But you were as silent as I was. The effect was as if you had been insulted, outrageously insulted by me. You're good at that. You never fail.

Two identical taxis drove up. I took the first one without waiting for you to let me go first. One behind the other we drove along beside the thrashing lake as far as Meersburg. I didn't look back. There was at least as much turbulence inside me as out there on the lake. The wild, stormy glitter on the high, arching waves matched my mood. Wave upon wave of harshly glistening cuirasses advanced in massive haste out of the west, as if somewhere there had been a battle of knights. On meeting the shore, the armored cavalcade of waves broke up, dissolving into foam and spume. Did you see that too? But without glasses you see much less than I do. And I had four pieces of eyeglasses at my disposal. Since I didn't look back I heard only later from Thiele that you took the taxi merely as far as Meersburg and waited there for a bus. I couldn't have done that. I needed the taxi all the way to Spellmann-Strasse, but on arriving there I found I didn't have my house key. Hilde was out with the girls at an amateur performance of some Mozart opera. I climbed up a ladder onto the balcony, but of course Hilde had locked all the doors and windows. So I had to sit in the dark on the terrace.

Suddenly I heard people coming around the house. Our neighbor with his four sons, all carrying flashlights. I didn't move, but they waved them around until I showed up in their beams. I didn't feel like offering any explanation. They apologized. They thought they had heard something. A metallic noise. As if someone had been trying to get into our house over the balcony. I merely said I hadn't heard anything, so they apologized again and withdrew in embarrassment. I should have thanked them for their vigilance and trouble. One must consider oneself lucky to have such neighbors. And I coldly dismiss those kind, helpful people, treating them as if they were brazen intruders, simply so I

can go on sitting in the dark while I reflect on the day
I've spent with you. And though I keep telling myself
not to dwell on it, so far I haven't stopped mulling
over this Ascension Day.

It was almost midnight by the time Hilde and the
girls came home. Fortunately, stimulated by their opera, all they wanted to do was hum and sing, and they
weren't in the least interested in me. Hilde didn't even
notice that at first I wasn't wearing any glasses at all
and later, indoors, was wearing my spare pair. Such is
the power of music over some people.

I must now point out that, in just under eight years,
you have resorted to violence four times, although on
two occasions you also harmed yourself. Let me remind you: 1) office picnic (pushed me off the bench
and then promptly stuck the carving fork in your arm);
2) in my house (overturned the table); 3) in Hamburg
(swept wineglasses off the table); 4) Haltnau (broke
eyeglasses, mine *and* yours). You will note that I am
not counting the watch-hurling incident in Hamburg.
But it is these acts of violence on your part that give
me hope. They tell me that there is more to you than
your trifling and fooling and teasing, your seemingly
imperturbable and invulnerable flippancy. Inside you
there is also a man with a grievance. I hope. I keep
hoping. I am still hoping. Perhaps it *is* merely a grievance that gives you so much weight, such a charismatic
quality. You are harboring (perhaps) a grievance that is
more serious than anything I've ever encountered myself. Mrs. Brass claims to have heard that you have

applied for an injunction against your wife to deny her
the right to bear your name; your children were also to
be denied that right. Why in hell—you're supposed to
have said—should you permit the use of your name by
people who wish to have nothing to do with you, who
are in fact obviously ashamed of you? As it was, you
had always objected to extending the use of names to
other people. If names were to have any meaning at all,
they couldn't simply be dumped on other people without injury to one or the other: the name or the other
person. So goes the rumor about you. Is it an expression of your increasing isolation, or is it the peak of
your insistence on being right? Perhaps the presence of
others can only pollute the degree of moral purity you
aspire to. Enough to send your narcissism into convul-
sions. Or you are simply the loneliest, the purest, of
all. Incompatible.

I am continuing to collect Liszt material. Mrs. Brass
is aware of this. Mrs. Brass says you're a radical. She
says that's what she likes about you, that you're such a
radical. It's nonproductive, she says, but one must be
glad that something of the kind still exists.

Did you at least do what, in our exuberance, we decided to do as we passed that Hagnau villa? Did you
scan the newspaper on Friday and Saturday for a report
on a gentleman of the retired-admiral type, a resident
of Hagnau who had killed his wife or daughter? Well,
what do you say now? It *was* the wife! Actually he
wasn't an admiral but a professor, and he didn't kill his
wife but got killed himself. Or were you totally unaware that a Professor Romualdo Marx was found

dead in his villa in Hagnau? And not only have they found no trace of his wife Gerhild, but the Marxes' motorboat is missing too. As I read that I was reminded of Professor Eggteil's thrice-uttered "Fuck Donald Duck!" Now it would seem that what he actually said was "Fuck Romuald Marx."

Shouldn't we go to the police together? But since after the first minute we would only be contradicting one another because you would go on insisting that the woman was a daughter, our statements would merely compound the confusion.

Is young Professor Eggteil still alive, I wonder? I believe so. He may well be unaware that old Professor R.M. is dead. She hasn't told the young professor about this. Or she ran so quickly past the man she had pushed down the stairs that she didn't realize the consequences. She merely wanted out—out of her prison. She's not alive anymore either. So I believe. The young professor appears to me—speaking as a clairvoyant—to have been orphaned. That woman drowned, I tell you. Eggteil saved himself, returned to the metropolis, and is teaching away there. The only thing I can imagine him being is an Anglicist. He teaches in order to forget, if you follow me. To forget the boating accident. That Gerhild insisted on joining him on the boat. Her husband tries to bar her way, she pushes him over and goes to pick up Eggteil. She welcomes the apocalyptic light of the lake. The whirling storm-warning lights all around excite her. Scarcely have she and her Eggteil moved out a bit into the lake when she wants something from him, and before you know it she loses her grip on the helm, a wave breaks over them from the stern, the luxury object sinks like a stone. Eggteil is roused abruptly from his aubergine fantasy. He thrashes about. Then he swims. All his reactions are more vigorous than he would have given himself credit for. He swims and swims, the waves carry him to shore, only now does he realize that Gerhild is missing. His suit dries on him and now looks much the same as it did before. He hasn't even lost a shoe, we hope. He walks to the railway station. In the dining car all he wants is water. He's never been so thirsty in his life.

From now on, Gerhild is present in all his lecture rooms. He watches as she develops a humpback. And her head begins to acquire a porcine look. Professor Eggteil, who has no Lord Liszt to whom he could confess everything, does have someone who recommends a psychoanalyst. The Gerhild-presence begins to subside, Eggteil lives to be ninety, but he dies in a bathtub, and in his hands they find an aubergine. Nobody can figure out what that means.

O.K.?

Here is another report from the local section of the newspaper, which, since it isn't in English, you wouldn't bother to read but which I have found interesting.

A MYSTERIOUS DISCOVERY

Last Friday some water-sports enthusiasts came upon two wooden statues drifting in the lake near the island

of Mainau. The Konstanz water police were sum-
moned to the scene, where they succeeded in salvaging
the two statues. Since the statues clearly depicted saints,
they were shown to Dr. Margrit Früh, director of the
historical collection of the Cantonal Museum. An ex-
pert from the Swiss National Museum in Zürich was
also consulted.

According to the experts' opinion, these statues date
from the baroque period and were carved by a Neapoli-
tan master or one of his pupils; the inserted glass eyes
support this theory. In all probability the statues rep-
resent Sigisbert and Placidus, the two patron saints of
the Upper Grisons. The position of the hand of one
saint, who is wearing the garb of an abbot, would seem
to indicate that he had been holding the model of a
church, probably the abbey of Disentis. From the close-
fitting hose worn by the other saint it may be inferred
that the statue is that of a layman. An abbot and a
layman: this points to St. Sigisbert and St. Placidus.
The unfinished backs of the statues indicate that they
must have originally stood against a wall. It has not yet
been established whether the statues were deliberately
thrown into the lake, or whether they fell into the water
while being transported.

Any persons having further information are re-
quested to contact the nearest police station.

Saints are no doubt frequently found floating around in
our lake. But now those particular two! As I read
about it, envy stirred in me. I envied Sigisbert and

Placidus. How harmoniously they must have floated side by side through all the storms for them to be espied and rescued together! Two wooden statues dating from the seventeenth century achieve this remarkable feat. Perhaps they entered the lake by way of the Rhine directly from the mountains of the Upper Grisons, borne peaceably along by the river's current through the length of the lake until they managed to veer away from the current as it emerges from the lake to end in cascades and annihilation. Then on they drift toward the garden isle of Mainau. And the glass eyes were still in place! On both statues, my lord! Abbot Sigisbert, you; Placidus, me. . . .

But the fact that one of us has recommended psychoanalysis to the other disqualifies us from the harmony of those mountain saints. So I assume that these two statues must represent the true couple of that particular day: Gerhild and Viktor. Mightn't Gerhild have carried the two statues from the villa onto the boat, intending to sell them in Switzerland, where St. Sigisbert and St. Placidus are popular, and use the money to live with Viktor? Anyway, should Eggteil never reappear and thus be presumed drowned, the couple would have first claim on the saintly manifestation. Gerhild-Sigisbert and Viktor-Placidus—may the Lord grant them eternal rest, may the Lord let them rest in peace. In response to your saga recitals, may I report that the erstwhile murderer of the gentle, beauteous Placidus was called Viktor; he was the boss of the city of Chur. And it all happened 1,259 years ago. In other words, our Viktor turned his hand against himself by taking up with Gerhild. Gerhild is lethal, no doubt about that.

Mightn't it be possible to believe that this Ascension Day, if only on account of its changing weather, tested us all? I failed the test.

This is the first time I have betrayed my inability to forget and forgive you for your part in my professional fate. What offended you, apparently, was that I dared to speak to you the way one speaks to a person who can no longer injure one because that person is even worse off than oneself. I yelled at you in my croaky voice. Why don't you write to me now? But then why am I writing to you? I like you, I almost said. I'd rather say: I'm quite sure I don't like you. Not anymore. How can you bear not to write to me! Considering you're in the right! You, the injured party, you could have written to me! Prompted by the satisfaction of someone who has suffered an injustice. But no! You keep me dangling, cast aside. . . . You're the most accomplished monster I've ever known. You are . . . I won't give you the satisfaction of another attack of truth on my part! Because that's what you got in Haltnau. I told the truth. I take back nothing, but I regret everything. Through your silence you are proving that in our relationship you alone are permitted to tell the truth. Year after year I said only that which would benefit our relationship. I could sense what you wanted to hear, and I said it. That's me all over. Truth: what is it, after all? I had a pretty good idea of what you did not care to hear, and I would keep it to myself.

It made me happy to tell you what made *you* happy. You always said whatever you happened to be thinking. You didn't indulge me. I told you nothing new in Haltnau. All I did was finally confess how I had felt throughout all these years about the way you treated me. All I did was quote the remarks you made in the third year, the fourth, the fifth. . . . And you didn't deny any of it, either. Sometimes you even sent me carbon copies of your remarks about me. If there's one thing foreign to your nature, it's intriguing behind a person's back. That's much more like me than like you. Those remarks I reminded you of in Haltnau— you could have taken them back, you could have said: It's true I did say such-and-such or write such-and-such five or six years ago, but by now I know better, I'm sorry, and anyway I now consider it presumptuous to judge another person in that way. . . . You did nothing of the kind. For a while you made a joke of it, then you were obviously shocked because I dared condemn you without immediately retracting. For the first time you were hearing how odious I'd found you through all those years. *That* was the shock. This fellow Horn is presuming to have disapproving thoughts! What's more, he's been keeping them to himself. For years. To one's face he seems friendly enough, but deep inside he reeks of resentment. Yes, even loathing.

So much for Haltnau. Enough's enough. I wish you all the best. That far I can go. I would prefer to have nothing more to do with you. Since returning to my family I feel better able to cope with things. I cannot end on an unambiguous note. You regard your decisiveness as a moral plus. You rank yourself on the very highest level, and you let others feel it. I liked you in spite of that. You liked me too, you will say. That's true only to the extent that you liked the person who promptly adjusted to you, but as soon as the real me emerged it was all over. You merely valued the product of my mimicry, which was far more your product than mine. So there, too, you loved only yourself, moral narcissist that you are. You are a superlative that constantly increases. By which I mean your capacity for intimidation.

I withdraw. I will continue to practice the state of separation. I want my life to be pleasant. To achieve that, I am willing to accept a somewhat empty room. Oh, my lord. I can't stop. I'm already too exhausted to be able to tear myself away. Writing is now my substitute for everything. Cramped handwriting in an otherwise empty room. Thiele could have been the friend I might have had. If he hadn't happened to be my boss. You would be a friend if you weren't a rival. The only two men with whom I might have been friends are disqualified from friendship by a crucial factor. It's too late now to set things right. You could, if you wanted to, find out from people who knew me twenty-five years ago that I used to get along with everyone. It was impossible to pick a quarrel with me. Now I'm approaching you in that guise, too. As the great peacemonger. But meanwhile you are right in your judgment: I've quarreled with everyone.

Perhaps those who found fault with me have changed me in a way they never intended. One hears that some children don't behave any better for being beaten. Now I've also started to approve of myself to the hilt. Now I can behave toward others as they used to behave toward me. To a T. I can now do only what I have learned. Whatever I did instinctively turned out to be wrong. I had to get rid of all that. Now I am what others have made of me. I can present myself to the world with a grin. There you have me. That's how you wanted me. I don't always find it easy to approve of myself. Especially in the morning, when I see myself in the mirror. Each night engraves itself with new strokes of the sickle. Each morning it becomes more difficult to restore that night-bruised face to a shape fit to show in the office. Each day I am one step farther down. But in the office I still have to appear on the step onto which once, long ago, I managed to boost myself. If I don't watch out, I feel as if I had just been spat upon. Or how else would you describe it, Lord Liszt? Oh, my lord, the only way I can cope with my propensity to exonerate myself is to stop. Moreover, I see with annoyance: the tip of the finger I am pointing at you is bending back toward me.

F.H.

P.S. XI

Oh, my lord, strictly speaking it's like this: my summer suits are more unprepossessing than my winter ones, and my winter suits are more unprepossessing than my summer ones. Yet another frustration you don't share with me.

F.H.

P.S. XII

Oh, my lord, strictly speaking death is a friend. It is not nothing, as many people believe. It is someone who takes us unmistakably by the hand and leads us out of the torture machine that we are obliged to use on one another. Everyone is—thoughtlessly—in favor of a world that is so bearable that death would be something terrible. As soon as I imagine such a world, I immediately feel warm and comfortable in the present one because in this world life is such that death is a welcome hand. Of course it is wrong of me to try to interfere. There is not the slightest danger of my ever committing such nonsense again. Nevertheless, I enjoy looking back on the attempt. It was a unique experience of a trend: everything one feels about oneself becomes a direction. One is a movement toward a small exit, but with no fear of not getting through. One can feel everything contracting inside, feel oneself becoming fantastically concentrated, caught up in an ever swifter current. Through that concentration one becomes darker. Speed and concentration increase to the point where one sees oneself moving away as a kind of projectile. And, whether you believe it or not, the final sensation was: this projectile is flying into the light. And even if this flesh, condemned as it is to sheer continuance, resists with every fiber, the last sigh will be a sigh of relief. So I believe.

F.H.

P.S.XIII

O.K. then, that's all, the end. Let's leave it at that: hostility is the only relationship we have achieved without effort. And the worse off an enemy is, the more we tend to like him. When things were going badly for me, I noticed that people were nicer to me. People like it when things go badly for someone else. More precisely: men do. Don't women also feel more comfortable with less beautiful women?

Now that things are looking up for me, I am once again aware of my normal sense of distance or, where proximity is unavoidable, hostility. Not another word against hostility, my lord! Our hostility is more intimate than any friendship I know. Or do you feel that's going too far? I leave it entirely up to you. Nothing brings tears to my eyes anymore. Nothing real. My response has changed. Now I cry only at the movies. My sensibilities respond only to stagecraft, to the total phoniness with which life is invariably presented on the screen. Penniless lieutenant falls in love after the war with millionairess; in America; amasses a fortune in a somewhat dubious manner; can now afford anything; would get the girl but she kills another woman in a car accident; her husband says: it was that stinking-rich guy; so the victim's husband goes and shoots first the lover, then himself; and all this in two or three hours. Shakes me to the core, something like that does. Stays with me, too. Thiele says no matter how often he sees a movie, to him it's always the first time. Movies never have any effect on him. But then of course he doesn't believe anything, no clinkers remain. His digestive process functions there too. I am brimful of movies. I am in their power. My soul seethes and steams like the sewage plant in New York. If only I could turn my back on myself! Turn entirely toward movies! My insensitivity toward the living is still incomplete.

Taking a shower: I can recommend that too. Forehead against the tiles, letting the hot water flow over one. Where else can one find as much tenderness as under a shower! And there are other satisfactions, my dear lord. I have just taken an empty cartridge out of my ballpoint and replaced it with a new one. That was most satisfying. The Austro-Finn should have brought us closer together. Oh, how we muffed that opportunity!

F.H.

P.S. XIV

Good morning, my lord. My third bottle of wine is empty. I am swaying a little. But only enough to avoid hitting anything. I sway to avoid clashes. It's your swaying that I'm imitating. It can be called inspired swaying. I take leave of you on a painless level. It is nearly five-thirty. I'm ready to leave for Bodnegg, I'll be there in less than an hour. Tomorrow is my mother's name day. But because tomorrow, Whit

Sunday, Hilde will be singing *Exaltavit spiritus meus in Deo salutari meo,* we are celebrating St. Klothilde's Day today. I wonder what I was thinking whenever Hilde's music room reverberated during the last few weeks with *Deposuit potentes de sede et exaltavit humiles?*

In Bodnegg there will be a soup, my lord, a soup such as you never dreamed of. A beef soup with dumplings and noodles, its soupiness overpowered by a thick green layer of herbs, mostly chives. It will be a soupy mush, but some clear broth can be added to each soup plate from the tureen. Oh, my lord, I'm happy now! I've put it all behind me. We have parted. I shall rush into the arms of my family. I'm glad to be alive. June is already glowing on the brow of the Allgäu. On June Saturdays, Bodnegg is permeated with the aromas of hay and soup. And each little place I drive through on the way there flaunts its peonies. Those peonies with their red and their white are, so to say, loud flowers. As if they were talking to one. "For your sake," that's the mood. Actually they're shouting, those peonies. So for the next hour or so I'll expose myself to the shouts of peonies. That's why I'm driving to Bodnegg. I almost said: forever. No, no, I'll be back. Trusty, resilient, a procurator of the unspoken.

F.H.

P.S. XV

I'm sorry. I don't mean to brag. Perhaps you should read this someplace where you can be alone for a while. I'm incapable of bragging. Of course I'm glad to be alive. But in Bodnegg we'll be sitting warily around a historic soup, trying to discern from my mother's vital signs how she would like us to behave today. In September she will be seventy-six, and to her everything is a disaster: past, present, and future. Above all, the future. She feels sorry for all those who have yet to experience what still lies ahead. For herself she wants everything, only not to die. She still hasn't told me who my father was. All Willi Horn gave me was his name. She married him so she wouldn't always have to face the world as Miss Zürn with a child. She fled from the lake up into the Allgäu with me so her parents wouldn't find out that she had a child before she had a husband. I was never allowed to go to Wigratsweiler while my grandparents were still alive. Although Klothilde Zürn did marry Willi Horn, my grandparents would obviously have noticed right away that I was almost two years older than the marriage. During his lifetime my Father Horn was given a pretty rough time by my mother. But then those who marry into this clan are never, as I now know, accorded full status. Willi, though, was actually made to suffer for his kindness in playing the role of my father. For her he was apparently never more than a substitute husband. The more members of the clan were present, the worse she treated him. I only hope that, when she was alone with him, she made up for it. I can't be sure.

In her I sense the toughness of another age. It may even have left its mark on me that, during the final eleven weeks of her pregnancy, she slept in the bed of one of her sisters and for eleven weeks never left that room. I was told this by the aunt with whom she found refuge. For eleven weeks that sister secretly carried my mother's excretions to the privy. The aunt kept house for their brother, but even he wasn't allowed to know that one sister had taken in the other. It was from that aunt, too, that I found out how and where I was born. But I'm not letting on about that.

Don't get me wrong: we are quite happy. Hilde will be singing with the girls. Sacred music. *Et nunc, et semper.* Sometimes I think my father's identity is kept from me because he was a priest. Such are the princeling-fantasies we indulge in hereabouts! Don't say: How would a priest get involved with a waitress? Every funeral is followed by a feast. The priest is cordially invited to partake, does so, the atmosphere of mourning does not survive the roast, the wine gets the better of the priest, the waitress sees herself as one of the elect, and there is one more witness to the flesh.

You can hardly consider *that* "bragging." I certainly don't want to be bragging as I part from you.

F.H.

P.S. XVI

As Jacob said when he wrestled with a man until the breaking of the day: "I will not let thee go, except thou bless me." So I must part from you without redress. I must be independent. In other words, it is *I* who must tell myself what is necessary. Let's imagine a person whose opinion of himself is shared by no one else. For years he blindly hopes that one day the world will think of him exactly as he thinks of himself. Things will happen, he hopes, to his advantage. He has visions of great feats. He's sure he will accomplish what is necessary. But then one accomplishment after another fails to materialize. Time after time that person disappoints himself. But he won't allow the world to be disappointed in him. The world must react according to his vision. So now it looks as if the world has failed, not he.

Imagine, if you can, everyone taking a man of my age for Franz Horn, while this same Franz Horn is debating whether he should take himself for Robert Bosch or Nietzsche. Shouldn't I also try to take myself for Franz Horn? I can command myself to do so, but I cannot summon the strength to obey such a command. I am surprised to find that not everyone has the same problem as I have. I hope that others have at least a similar problem. It would be terrible if I were the only one. It would be terrible if everyone had that problem. No one can identify with the person he is in the eyes of others. But until he declares himself identical with the person he is for others he doesn't have a moment's peace. That's how it is with me. Every second one may face punishment for the discrepancy between one's own image and reality. Reality is what counts. Reality is what the others say.

I wanted to make first Thiele, then you, an accomplice in appropriating reality by stealth. I wanted to bribe first Thiele, then you. I wanted to persuade you both to regard my self-image as the true one. I failed. First with Thiele, then with you. There you have it. Is that enough? May I go now? I'll say no more. Is there any more? Oh, yes. But not until the day when, staggering and lurching rather than walking, you work your way across the factory yard, not until alcohol has really got the better of you: not until then will I tell you more about me. So I am watching your downfall with sympathy and impatience. I am waiting for you. You are still much too high up for me. Not in reality, only in your self-estimation! In reality you are, I believe, almost within reach. But your sense of self! That air of patronizing superiority! That bulwark of illusions! I can wait, my lord. Your failure in the firm will become apparent on the day of the merger, if not before. I am convinced that the McKinsey consultant will be examining the questionnaires you hand in for their alcohol content. And why does Thiele allow you to dawdle along like this? Because he knows that, come January, he will be rid of you as well as of me and, with young people from all over Europe, will be producing the finest floats in the world in his Fin Star Company. No conglomerate can tolerate us two, my lord. Not the two of us. My lack of success is a known quantity. Your failure is still to be demonstrated. Your failure will be my success. Which brings us to the sixth and final law of our six laws of physics: the failure of his rival is the success of the unsuccessful.

F.H.

P.S. XVII

Oh, my lord, I would much rather not have written all that. But I felt compelled to do so. By you. Can you understand that? Let us finally unburden ourselves as much as we can instead of suffering like bumblebees. Or aren't you suffering at all? Does the one who is in the right not suffer? Does *everything* serve to gratify you? Even your downfall? That most of all? May you enjoy it! (Please feel free to imagine a few of these sentences being shouted in my croaky voice.) I have not succeeded tonight in making you smaller than you want to be. Laughing, relaxed, powerful, and resilient: that's your reaction to whatever I find it in me to say. You have eluded me. Now I am out of breath, all out of strength. Your behavior toward me is one of divine capriciousness. And whatever you do or don't do in total arbitrariness, you invariably hit my tenderest spot. With consummate skill. Or how else would you describe it, Lord Liszt?

I hope I haven't been reproaching you. I am brimful with the knowledge that we are all equal. (Egalitarian is what you should call me, not hierarchist.) There is nothing more grotesque than someone reproaching someone else. I no longer love you. Especially when you're not around. But I blame myself for this, not you.

I won't make myself any clearer. I need the half-light. That's why I always mix enough darkness with light so that, however carefully I look, I see less than I can bear. Horn's policy, my lord. After all, I don't want to see myself, in my relationship to you, as some poor girl of the nineteenth century. Go on doing whatever you like. I'll soon feel like Mrs. Brass: my hopes are vested in the merger. I apologize for finally invoking reality to come to my aid against you.

> *Yours sincerely,*
> *F.H.*

P.S. XVIII

Oh, my lord, I can't make amends. Nor would I want to. Not even for the sake of regaining a reputation for sanity. I'd rather be lying prone mumbling deliriously into the inaudible. I mean it. Meet the paranoiac, meet the catastrophist, meet the loser. Or how else would you describe me, Lord Liszt? Come now, my dear Franz. . . . No.

> *F.H.*

P.S. XIX

Oh, Lord Liszt, I feel fine now.

I insist that you believe this.

At the moment I see myself as a relaxed optimist.

The extent of my defeat goes beyond anything I can feel. So I'm in luck.

Is anyone *not* sheer filth?

The main thing is to perceive one's debris as a shield and weapon.

Anything good between us is no longer possible.

These scars remain wounds.

And even if, with the best of intentions, we were to make peace, we will never again reach a state in which we cease to harm one another.

And I regret that so much.

I really do, Lord Liszt.

How many times can a confession be repeated before it becomes a lie?

I feel so deserted: a condition that accentuates everything. Including perception. Otherwise I would feel less deserted.

I feel I am the poorer by an experience.

Your truly relaxed
Horn

FRANZ HORN threw his pen out the window. The movement triggered a flash of pain from his fingers all the way up his arm into his spine, so stiff was he with tension. But he was also feeling so wrought up and impassioned that he welcomed any pain. He felt capable of relishing any pain. He wanted that pain to go on and on! Had he ever been as alive as at this moment? Wasn't he on fire? All the places that hurt released images of fire. His headache prompted the notion that hot rails were running through his head, red-hot rails with flashing images racing along them. He thought: You feel like an oyster splashed with a drop of lemon juice and waiting for the master's tongue. When he tried to turn his head, a point in the nape of his neck responded with a sharp pain and he had to press one hand against that point to be able to turn his head slightly. He felt exhausted. But at the same time it was a good feeling. He hadn't felt that good for a long time.

He undressed, stepped into the shower, leaned his forehead against the tiles, and let the hot water flow over him. So long as he was free to do that, he had no cause for complaint. Drying oneself in the oversize bath towel was probably another sinful privilege of a Central European. He saw in the mirror that, in picking up the ball caster, he had scraped his forehead against the windowsill. The skin around his eyes reminded him of circus elephants. They had that look. That lugubrious expression. He thought: That fellow in the mirror is aging faster than I am.

He dressed. Put on all clean clothes. Then back to his desk. He would rather not have gone back, but tomorrow Hilde would be coming home from her singing. Under no circumstances must she see what he had written. The thought of her reading that was agonizing. Yet he couldn't send off the letter either. He must stop thinking of what he had written to Liszt. He wanted to forget about it. How disgusting, to have exposed himself like that! There was only one thing left: the fireplace. He picked up the sheets and went out onto the terrace, remembering to take along the matches. Hilde would see he had been burning something. He could remove the ashes and prepare a new pile of twigs and branches all ready for lighting so that the outdoor fireplace would once again look exactly as it did now. But what would the neighbors think if he lit a fire on Whit Saturday before seven in the morning? TV thriller. There was no way he could burn his letter to Lord Liszt.

Franz Horn went back to his desk and stuffed the written pages into the left bottom drawer. That was where they belonged. He pushed them underneath everything else stored in the drawer. He didn't want his eyes to fall immediately on those pages each time he opened the drawer. If he could have had his wish, he would at this moment have liked to do some target practice with a pistol, using that obnoxious drawer as a target. He could actually visualize the drawer being splintered, ripped apart, by the bullets. He was forever dreaming up pseudo-solutions: he was a TV person.

If he left now he would be in Bodnegg before breakfast. Maybe he could climb over the garage roof and the balcony into the room where Hilde was sleeping, get into bed beside her, and move his hand toward her so she would grasp it in her half-sleep and draw it close like something she had just rescued.

He emptied the ashtrays that he had filled during the night, rinsed and put away his glass, and removed the empty bottles. It pleased him to think that the house now contained three bottles less of that Lord Liszt wine. He had the feeling of having worked hard. He was tired, but his mood was better than any he had shown or described in his letter to Liszt. The hardest thing, it seemed, was to convey some idea of the true tolerability of one's own life. Reports of disaster, despair: no trick to that. He didn't feel he had lied, but once again he had been overconsiderate of Liszt's alleged miserable state. He had crept up on that state. He had summoned up the very thing that was bound to ingratiate himself with that ruthless man of morality: a confession. He hadn't dared to admit how happy he could feel. He had said nothing of his strength. No one would ever have the least inkling of how much he could keep back in talking to others. Or did that apply to everyone? Did everyone show merely the tip of the iceberg? Were there only icebergs communicating with each other, hiding the greater part of themselves? He should have at least hinted that much to Dr. Liszt. After reading the letter, Liszt would once again simply believe that he knew all about Franz Horn. Other people had no idea of the true distance Franz Horn knew how to maintain. He remembered, for example, the prostate remedy he had been given by his Uncle Chrystostomus. He didn't need anything like that just yet. But his uncle had told him that, having no children of his own, he wanted his favorite nephew, Franz, to inherit this remedy, known only to himself. If applied in such-and-such a way this simple natural product was a guaranteed aid. Uncle Chrystostomus could never be accused of bragging. So the remedy must be reliable. When Horn happened one day to learn from a remark of Thiele's that the latter was already having some trouble in this area, he was tempted to hand over the remedy to him. But he restrained himself. Keep your distance! he had shouted at himself deep below the surface. None of those others would credit him with such self-control. And that was precisely what pleased him whenever he thought of it. As soon as one of those others proved to be a friend, Horn would be only too glad to pass along the remedy.

What had happened to that ball caster? Where had he

put it? Where was he likely to have put it? He hadn't been out to the shed yet. So where could he have put it down temporarily after picking it up from under the radiator? Those were his favorite problems. He knew at once that he must have placed the ball caster on something soft or at least some fabric so it wouldn't slip off, and at eye level too, and on the way to the door into the garden. So all he had to do was follow his normal route to the garden, and he would find it. He started off. There it was, lying on the sofa arm to the left of the door, in full view.

He walked out to his shed. To his creation. Every board, every beam, had been sawed, fitted, screwed, and nailed into place with his own hands. He opened the door, and there was his collection, his *omnium-gatherum,* looking at him. Every fender, every lamp-shade, every piece of corrugated iron, every hinge . . . he knew precisely how, when, and where he had picked up each item. Now, whenever he came across the ball caster in here he would be able to relive the day he had brought it home. From the tribute to the deceased Stierle to the ending of his letter to Lord Liszt, including the bump on his head. Those were his mile-stones. It seemed to him that each one of them was more exceptional than the milestones of the world, than, say, the impending visit of the pope to Poland, which everyone was talking about at the moment. That his milestones were so unimportant corre-sponded to his own unimportance. Right on, as the rising young executives would say. So: Where would be the best place to put the ball caster now? There wasn't an inch of space. The shed had been crammed to the roof for a long, long time. For every new object for which he wanted to find a spot, he had to pick up a hundred others and rearrange them more closely, more ingeniously. That was the glorious part about it. The result was an ever-increasing density of objectification. He quickly realized that this was not the moment to indulge in his favorite pastime. He found a makeshift place for the ball caster between a coaster hub and a ball faucet.

Too bad that Hilde was incapable of appreciating the inherent order in the placing of all these objects. Come to think of it, at VW's death Franz's mother had taken her husband's entire collection and handed it over to the garbage men. Franz Horn hadn't been aware of this until he helped his mother move. His own *omnium-gatherum* would suffer precisely the same fate. That's fine with me, he thought. At the moment he was able to admit to himself that the self-control he required to drive along a street on one of those days set aside for the city to collect discarded furniture, etc., was as unreliable as Hilde believed. Only too often, unfortunately, he would suddenly stop the car, run back past two or three houses, and, with a guilty conscience— i.e., afraid of being caught—drag the frame of a lawn chair back to the trunk of his car. Hilde had caught him at it one day and, in her most strident manner, forbidden him to add junk of that sort to his collection. If she ever caught him at it again . . . she might really move out. His rows with Hilde were pretty grisly affairs if only because of the difference in their voices. Hilde's shrill screams, his croaky abuse. No doubt the neighbors interpreted their quarrel as a frenzied monologue on Hilde's part punctuated by inexplicable pauses.

He went back into the house. Why shouldn't he do his vocal exercises before driving to Bodnegg? A day without exercises was a dead day was what his speech therapist had dinned into him with the force of her own magical, sonorous voice.

He took out his voice-exercise book, opened it at page 59, and articulated: *sick, seek, sicken.* . . . For ten minutes. Then another ten minutes of "exhalation exercises" according to Fernau-Horn: *hole, home, host.* . . . His voice was improving. All he needed was motivation. He was motivated. If he ever ran into Liszt or Thiele sometime in the future, they would be surprised.

His exercises over, he couldn't restrain himself any longer: he dialed Liszt's number. But as he dialed the first digit a black spider darted out from under the rotating disk. He dropped the receiver. He stood up. The spider had disappeared. He replaced the receiver, picked it up again, dialed. Horst Liszt answered immediately. So he must also be at his desk already. However, instead of giving his name he simply said, "Yes?" A deep, calm, noncommittal yes. Horn was tongue-tied. He wanted to say: Good morning. But he couldn't. Liszt went on: "Oh well, if you've changed your mind, that's your privilege." Liszt replaced the receiver. Horn had a feeling that Liszt knew who had phoned him. He could feel himself blushing. Off to Bodnegg, this very minute! Otherwise he might get the notion that he couldn't leave the house. He was feeling very comfortable now. The letter to Lord Liszt hadn't sapped his strength! And not sending it hadn't either! In future, whenever there was some person whom he mistakenly believed to be essential to himself, he would write him a night letter like that, one that it would be impossible to send. There's nothing better than that!

While walking from the front door to the car, he couldn't understand what had happened to him the evening before halfway between front door and car. As he walked toward the car now, his eyes were fixed on the garden poppies, which last evening had still been quite inconspicuous in the little front garden but had fully opened during the night. Compared with wild poppies, he found his garden poppies looked obscene. Monstrous. But that suited him perfectly. Poppy, poppy, poppy, Franz Horn thought, you're a reminder that I am alive. Maybe that's a good thing after all. One might, for instance, laugh or cry for sheer June: the birds certainly sounded as if they were reveling in it. The vibrating, twittering fabric left no empty spaces. In any event, wearing his clean socks and his sandals he walked toward his car and, almost light-headed with composure, drove out onto the street. He was on his way to a party. He had no problems. The void hummed intriguingly. And ahead of him the Allgäu wore the sun like a diadem.